WHERE EUROPE BEGINS

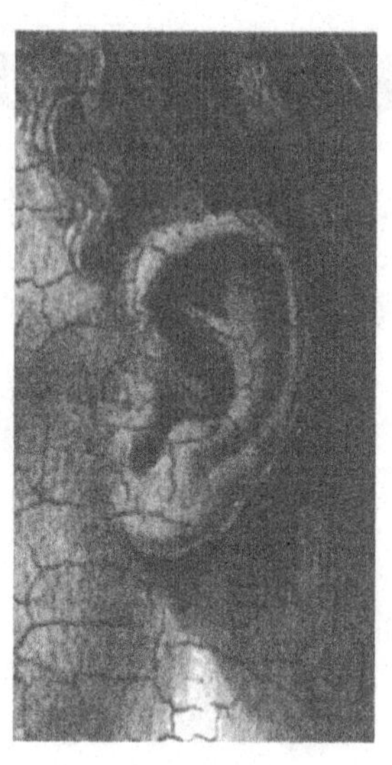

WHERE EUROPE BEGINS

Yoko Tawada

Translated from the German by
SUSAN BERNOFSKY
from the Japanese by
YUMI SELDEN

WITH A PREFACE BY WIM WENDERS

A NEW DIRECTIONS BOOK

Some of these stories first appeared in the following magazines: "Canned Foreign" and "The Talisman" in *Fiction International 24*; "Raisin Eyes" in *The Transcendental Friend* (www.morningred.com) 10; "Storytellers without Souls" (excerpt) in *Two Lines 2001*; "Where Europe Begins" in *Conjunctions 33*.

All of the stories in this volume except "Spores" were originally published in German in various collections brought out by konkursbuch Verlag Claudia Gehrke PF 1621, 72006 Tübingen.

Manufactured in the United States of America
New Directions Books are printed on acid-free paper.
First published clothbound by New Directions in 2002 and as New Directions Paperbook NDP1079 in 2007

Library of Congress Cataloging-in-Publication Data
Tawada, Yoko, 1960–
Where Europe begins / Yoko Tawada ; translated from the German by Susan Bernofsky ; from the Japanese by Yumi Selden ; with a preface by Wim Wenders.
p. cm.
ISBN 978-0-8112-1702-6 (alk. paper)
I. Bernofsky, Susan. II. Selden, Yumi, 1970– III. Title.
PT2682.A87 W44 2002
833'.914—dc21

2002005196

10 9 8 7

New Directions Books are published for James Laughlin
by New Directions Publishing Corporation
80 Eighth Avenue, New York, NY 10011

Contents

Translators' Note

Yoko Tawada's work straddles two continents, two languages and cultures. Born in Tokyo in 1960, she moved to Hamburg at the age of 22 and became, simultaneously, a German and a Japanese writer. She has since published a good ten volumes in each language, won numerous literary awards (including Japan's prestigious Akutagawa Prize in 1993 and, in 1996, Germany's Adelbert von Chamisso Prize, the highest honor bestowed upon a foreign-born author), and established herself, in both countries, as one of the most important writers of her generation.

Tawada's poetry, fiction, essays and plays return again and again to questions of language and culture, the link between national and personal identity. If the languages we speak help define us, what happens to the identity of persons displaced between cultures? "The interesting," she once said in an interview, "lies in the in-between." And so her characters are constantly in motion, journeying between countries, languages and modes of being—providing us with "travel narratives" full of glimpses into the interstices of the world in which the structure of all experience is revealed.

Of the stories contained in this volume, two ("The Bath" and "Spores") were written in Japanese, and the rest in German. Three of the shorter German pieces ("Storytellers without Souls," "Canned Foreign" and "The Talisman") appeared in the collection *Talisman,* which inspired the essay by Wim Wenders.

Tawada's most recent books in German are *Opium für Ovid* (*Opium for Ovid*) and *Überseezungen* (*Foreign Tongues*), and in Japanese, *Hinagiku no cha no baai* (*If It's Camomile*) and *Hikari to zerachin no raipuchihhi* (*The Leipzig of Gelatin and Light*). She was the Max Kade Writer in Residence in the German department at MIT in 1999, has had three plays performed on major stages in Germany and Austria, and has recently gone on a reading/performance tour with jazz pianist Aki Takase.

Preface:
On Yoko Tawada's *Talisman*

Reading this book,
I kept feeling a tremendous urge to take off my hat
    to the author.
As it happens, I wasn't wearing one
and I wasn't sitting on a subway, either,
where the book had just taken me,
but in an airplane.
Still, I had a desire to at least bow, if only in spirit.
Not the way we bow in Germany, of course,
with just the slightest nod of the head,
but in the Japanese style,
bending from the waist at a ninety-degree angle.
And I would hold this position for some time:
Only the most profound reverence, I felt,
could do justice to this writer and her work.

The book is a travelogue.
It relates the experiences of a traveler,
and as the reader you experience all sorts of things
yourself
and you travel far and wide while reading it.
Where do these travels take you?
Let me start this differently.

I am a great traveler myself,
have done quite a lot of writing in planes, trains
and hotels
and also made a number of films on the road.
I've been to Japan so often
that I can rightfully call it "countless times,"
and even recorded one of these visits in a diary film
called *Tokyo-Ga*.
Nonetheless, I've always remained an outsider,
a puzzled, marveling observer,
and, as I've come to realize,
the more time I spend in the country,
the less I know about it.
In the end, I'm still a tourist.

At least that's the impression I have
when I consider the reverse journey
that this Japanese woman

made into my own country, into Germany.

While all I managed to do in Japan
was to learn a handful of signs and phrases,
beyond which the language remained a book with
    seven seals for me,
Yoko Tawada has actually mastered the German
    language,
has actually studied and worked here,
and has indeed written this complex, subtle,
    intelligent and poetic book
in German!

An utterly heroic, even titanic task that she has taken
    upon herself,
it appears to me,
the more I immerse myself in it,
though there is nothing laborious about the book
    itself,
on the contrary, it flows effortlessly.

At the same time, this is definitely not a "German"
    book,
if I may put things in such simplistic terms.
No one else but a Japanese woman could have had
    these experiences

and could have written this book,
down to its grammar and its most minute
observations.

Above all, the book deals with these "small" observations,
even if this procedure gradually expands to a much
larger picture:
A voyage of discovery and adventure that transports
the reader
deep into what Yoko Tawada once called the *bretselhaft*
German soul
(in an untranslatable German adjective of her own
invention
that combines the words "mysterious" and "pretzel").
Like in a novel by Jules Verne,
fantastic new spaces keep opening up before your
inner eye,
and with conflicting emotions and mixed feelings
I rediscovered in its pages my fatherland and mother
tongue,
torn between tenderness, understanding and
indignation,
smiling and frowning again the next moment.

Having embarked on this adventure,
I learned so much about "us," about "ourselves,"

that I almost didn't realize,
when the journey came to an end,
that I suddenly knew far more about Japan
than I ever saw or learned there, "on location."

And it was here, at this intersection,
that I finally understood
what is so astonishing about this book:
It is not set in Rothenburg-on-the-Tauber,
not in Hamburg or Tokyo.
It is not a book about "Europe" versus "Asia" or the
other way around.
Rather, it is a book that comes to us from a no-
man's-land
where words, names, signs have no meaning any more,
a place where everything is put in question,
and where the only actions that count
are perceiving, taking in, feeling
and relating the experience of it all.

Thus, this slim volume suddenly becomes a model,
a model of utopian storytelling, of utopian traveling.
And so, as in my mind
there cannot possibly be a more beautiful book,
and I can't come up with more flattering
compliments,
I am holding my imaginary hat far in front of me,

almost touching the floor,
and I am looking forward,
at the end of this flight from Berlin to Los Angeles,
to all the things that I will be able to see differently,
in Japan as well as in Germany.
Thanks to this book by Yoko Tawada.

WIM WENDERS

I. THE BATH

THE BATH

1

Eighty percent of the human body is made of water, so it isn't surprising that one sees a different face in the mirror each morning. The skin of the forehead and cheeks changes shape from moment to moment like the mud of a swamp, shifting with the movements of the water below and the footsteps of the people walking above it.

I had hung a framed photograph of myself beside the mirror. The first thing I would do when I got up was to compare my reflection with the photograph, checking for discrepancies which I then corrected with makeup.

Compared to the fresh complexion shown in the photograph, the face in the mirror looked bloodless and pale, like the face of a dead person. Perhaps this is why the rectangular frame of the mirror reminded me of a coffin. When I held up the candle to look more closely, I saw that my skin was covered with fine, overlapping scales, smaller than the wings of tiny insects. Carefully I inserted one long thumbnail beneath a scale and flicked it off. In this way I was able to strip off the scales one at a time. When I unbuttoned my pajama top, I saw the scales covered not only my face but my chest and arms as well. If I began removing them one by one, I would be late for work. I decided to take a bath to soften the scales and then rub them off.

Once upon a time there was an impoverished village in a valley where no rice would grow. A pregnant woman was so hungry that when she found a fish one day she wolfed it down raw without sharing it with the other villagers. The woman gave birth to a lovely baby boy. Afterwards, her body grew scales, and she turned into an enormous fish. She could no longer survive on land, and went to live all by herself beneath the river. An old man took the child in. Boys have always swapped insulting comments about their mothers when they quarrel. "Your mother's a whore!" "Your mother doesn't have a belly-button!" They don't know what those things mean, but they say them anyhow. This boy heard the same contemptuous words over and over: "Your mother has scales!" One day the boy asked the old man what it meant to have scales, and where his mother really lived. Once he had discovered the secret of his origins, the boy could think of nothing but how to change his mother back into a human being. In the end, he decided to break open the rock of the surrounding mountains to irrigate the fields and make a rice paddy. The villagers' poverty would end if they could grow rice. The boy went to see his mother to tell her about his plans. She was very happy and wanted to help. The boy drew a map and decided where to break open the rock wall. His mother threw her large, scaly body against the rock again and again, and little by little it began to crumble. Day and night she threw herself against the rock. The scales that were scraped from her body flew up into the air and danced in the wind like blood-stained cherry petals. This is how the village, which had no cherry trees, came to be called the Village of Cherry Blossoms. Once they had irrigated fields, the villagers no longer had to starve, but the mother, who had lost all her scales and become human again, bled to death.

When I finished getting out of my pajamas, the phone rang. Still naked, I picked up the receiver. I didn't say anything, and from the other end of the line came a man's voice I had never heard before.

"It's you?"

I thought about this for a moment and said, "It isn't."

"If it's not you, then who are you?"

I put down the receiver. That was my first conversation on this strange day.

Slowly I got into the hot water, starting with my big toe.

As long as I don't move the water around, I can stand even very hot water. I closed my eyes, held my breath, and submerged myself entirely in the long bathtub. I thought: burial at sea is fine, a grave beneath the earth is fine, but not cremation—cremation I couldn't stand.

When I got out of the bath, the scales had softened. I scraped them off with a pumice stone. They came off with relatively little effort. I would have hated having to throw myself against a rock wall and die. It was a good thing I had no son.

When I returned to the mirror, the scales were gone, but on my nose I saw a large number of tiny blisters smaller than ants' heads. I popped one with my nail, and a greasy white substance came out. It smelled like rancid mayonnaise. Once I started I couldn't stop and popped one after the other. Outside I could hear the birds beginning to chirp and flap their wings. Unless I hurried I would really be late for work. When I had popped the last of the blisters, what remained was not smooth skin but a desolate desert landscape scattered with deflated balloons.

The telephone rang again. I picked up the phone and didn't say anything until the caller said, "Hello, it's me." It was a familiar voice.

"Excuse me, may I ask who's calling?" I couldn't help asking, even though I knew who it was.

"It's me," the man's voice said. "Is it all right if I come over tonight?"

"That would be fine, but I won't be home till late. You have the key?"

"I'm working late too, so I wouldn't have time earlier, anyway. See you then."

I wondered how I already knew I wouldn't be home till late.

I washed my face with white sand. This is the only way to smooth a skin that's become like a desert. This sand was supposedly made of whales' bones that had been tossed up by the sea and bleached in the sun. When I scooped some up in my palm and held it to my face, the sand spoke to my bones through my flesh. I distinctly felt the shape of my skull in my hand. Beyond a skin made of light and flesh made of water, there is another body. Only, as long as that body is alive, no one will be able to hold it close.

Sometimes other people's skulls look transparent. At such moments I fall in love.

When I had moistened my skin with milk lotion, the face in the mirror began to look like the face in the photograph. This lotion isn't a pharmaceutical product, it's made of real mother's milk. So it not only moisturizes the skin but also soothes the nerves and gives one energy.

I finished my makeup and combed my hair. In the grasslands of a dream, I painstakingly combed out the spores of poisonous mushrooms and the carcasses of winged insects. When I was a child, I never combed my hair. This was because it made me feel as though my head had just been emptied of its contents. It was not really the brain, but the hair, that did the thinking. At school the teachers always said to comb and braid your hair, probably because they were afraid of the children's hair. They say that hair has strange powers. In the old days, people used to cut a lock of hair to give to someone setting off on a journey, to ward off harm. They also used to touch foreigners' hair to cure illnesses.

Once, a long time ago, there was a village in which lived a gluttonous woman. She worked hard and had a good disposition, and so she was well-liked in the village, but she ate so many helpings of rice that her husband thought it strange. Moreover, she forbade others to watch her eat, and would take her meals alone at night in the barn. One night the man crept up to the barn to watch, and he saw that each of the woman's hairs had turned into a snake and was eating rice. Astonished, the man got out his rifle and shot the woman dead.

They say hair is the part of the skin that has died and hardened. Part of my body is already a corpse.

2

The photograph beside the mirror is one Xander took of me several years ago. He appeared before me one day with three Leica cameras slung over his shoulder. This was the first encounter between the photographer and his model. He explained that he was really an activist photographer, but he couldn't live on such little pay, so now he was working for a travel agency and had come to take pictures for an advertising campaign. He handed me a homemade business card. I didn't know how to pronounce the "X" in "Xander." Since it was the first letter of his name, I couldn't begin to speak at all. Xander was already squatting on the ground, unpacking his cameras and other equipment. My eyes were still crucified by the X. Until the day I learned Xander was short for Alexander, I was tormented by the question I had first encountered in my junior high school math book: "Find the value of x." If x was *durchein,* it meant *durcheinander* (mixed up); if it was *mitein,* then *miteinander* (together)—but I couldn't help suspecting there were even more horrifying words. When the camera's eye stared at me head-on, I turned away in embarrassment, as if I'd been caught gazing into a mirror. The bulb flashed. After that, only the black hole of the lens remained in my field of vision.

"Don't be afraid. The camera isn't a gun," Xander said. The lens was trying to trap me; my eyes turned into fish made of light and attempted to dart away through the air.

"Can't you look a little more Japanese? This is for a travel poster."

There was another flash. The camera was cutting time into thin slices, the way a knife slices ham. One can then pick up these slices one by one and look at them, or eat them. For pleasure, or as an alibi. But what did I need an alibi for? I didn't yet know I was going to become entangled in a homicide case.

"Keep your eyes on the lens," Xander said. The camera in front of me was an old-fashioned Leica. It kept trying to peer into my eyes, like a psychologist. If it wanted to learn my soul's secrets, I had nothing to worry about, since there weren't any. But this camera was trying to capture my skin.

"Relax," Xander ordered. The camera was gauging its target's position and distance.

"Smile," Xander said severely. I attempted to tighten my facial muscles into a smile, but didn't succeed. They say when you fall in love your face becomes distorted and you can no longer smile naturally.

"Why do you need to take so many?"

"It makes it more likely there's a good shot among them."

"Even with such a good camera, you can't take a good picture in one shot?"

"Don't talk. It's no good if you talk."

He might have been a dentist, unable to work while the patient is talking. The camera was part of the treatment. It was trying to preserve my body from death by burning it onto the paper. There was another flash.

"That should be enough," Xander said, lowering his

camera. When his face appeared where the camera had been, it looked very much like my own.

A few days later, Xander came over again with his camera.

"You didn't come out in any of the photographs," he said resentfully.

"Why? Was the camera broken?"

"The camera was fine. The background came out beautifully, but you aren't in any of the pictures."

For a little while, neither of us said anything.

"It's all because you don't have a strong enough sense of yourself as Japanese," he said.

I looked at him in surprise. "Do you really think skin has a color?"

Xander laughed. "Of course. Or do you think it's the flesh that's colored?"

"How could flesh possibly have color? There's color in the play of light on the surface of the skin. We don't have colors inside."

"Yes, but the light plays on your skin differently than on ours."

"Light is different on every skin, every person, every month, every day."

"Each one of us, on the other hand, has a special voice inside. There is..."

"There aren't any voices inside us. What you hear is air vibrating outside our bodies."

Xander thought for a little while. Then he looked up and said, "Would you mind if I tried makeup?"

Xander covered my face with a powder base. He laid it on so thickly that it closed up all my pores and my skin could no longer breathe. Then with a fine brush he traced the outlines of my eyelids, working as carefully as an archaeologist brushing bits of dirt from an earthenware shard he's excavating. Then he filled in the area where my mouth was with lipstick exactly the color of my lips.

"I'll dye your hair black for you."

"Why do you want to blacken hair that's already black?"

"Unless it's dyed, it'll come out white as an old woman's because of the flash."

"What if you don't use flash?"

"Then nothing will come out."

When he finished dying my hair, Xander drew an x on my cheek.

"When I was a child, I marked everything precious to me with an x, so it would belong to me." Then he kissed the mark.

After that Xander stood me in front of a wall and pressed the shutter release button as casually as if he were pulling a trigger. The x on my cheek dug into my flesh. It stopped the light from playing and crucified the image of a Japanese woman onto the paper.

3

I wasn't really a model, I was only a simultaneous interpreter who was uncertified and thus got very few assignments. Every day after completing my toilette, I would go to the office and wait for work. If by the end of the day I hadn't been called, I would go home without having done anything at all. But sometimes I did receive an assignment, and then I would have a sip of whiskey and go to work.

That morning, my office received a call from a Japanese firm that had arranged a luncheon for its German clients. The company exported machines that processed fish for canning, bones and all. I was to fill in for an interpreter who had fallen ill. The restaurant had a lakefront view and belonged to a famous hotel. On either side of the long table sat five members of each firm, like children playing a war game with two opposing teams. I was seated next to the president of the Japanese firm. He had slightly rounded shoulders and a habit of nodding emphatically. On the other side of the table sat the Germans, two women and three men. One of the women wore a blouse that exposed her shoulders. Another had on a tight skirt and sat with her long legs crossed. Both sat with their backs held straight and their chins thrust out, and when they blinked, they did so unhurriedly. When they looked down, lines appeared on either side of their mouths, and they looked bitter and exhausted from too much work, but this impression dissipated when they stuck out their chins a bit more.

On the Japanese side sat only middle-aged men in suits. Astonished, a long-faced man said in a low voice, "So the women here wear sexy clothing even to work." Since the silence had been broken, all the Germans turned toward me in curiosity. "What did he say?" one of them asked, apparently too excited to wait for me to speak of my own accord.

"He is admiring that old china and says it is indeed very fine," I said, translating a sentence no one had said.

When my work takes me to an exclusive restaurant, I always order sole. Sole, unlike flounder, never tastes bland, and it's also not fatty like salmon. I don't know anything more delicious in Western cuisine. But it's not just because of the taste I insist on sole. It's the word itself. Sole, soul, sol, solid, delicious sole of my soul; the *sole* reason I don't *lose* my *soul,* and my *soles* stand on a *solid* footing still... When I eat sole, I'm never at a loss for words with which to translate.

On this day, however, one large fish was ordered for the whole party, so I wasn't able to order sole.

When the waiter finished pouring the aperitifs, the president of the company gave a speech. "Ladies and gentlemen, we are very happy to welcome you here today." Head down, I began to translate mechanically. At the end of the sentence I looked up, and met the penetrating gaze of a Japanese man in metal-rimmed glasses. Interpreters are like prostitutes that serve the occupying forces; their own countrymen hold them in contempt. It's as if the German entering my ears were something like spermatic fluid. "There is an old saying that there is no such thing as an accidental meeting. It is nonetheless now our task to turn our meeting into something meaningful." The German at the right end of the table was staring at the president of the Japanese firm, trying to look interested, but he kept fidgeting under the table, obviously bored. "I earnestly hope we will have further opportunities to continue our association." Glasses clinked. The German at the left end of the table, a little younger than the others, raised his elbow and, like an actor in front of the mirror, slowly drained his glass. The long-faced Japanese man smacked his lips loudly and said, "What an excellent aperitif." The tight-skirted woman frowned and turned her head to look at him.

"Over here, you're not supposed to make noises at dinner," whispered the man in the metal-rimmed glasses.

"Oh, yes, so I've heard."

"The ladies don't like it when you make noise."

The president of the German firm looked over at me, expecting a translation.

"What kind of liqueur is this?" Again I translated a sentence no one had said. The German president looked pleased, and explained the notion of pre-dinner drinks. When I translated, the Japanese president looked bored and said, "Look, they sell these in Japan too. Now, let's talk about you," he added paternally. "Why are you living all by yourself in a place like this? You should go home and get married, or your parents will worry."

At this point, the master chef and his assistant carried in a large fish between them, as if they were carrying a wounded person on a stretcher out to an ambulance. The white, swollen belly of the fish looked like a fat woman's thigh, and perhaps because of this, the arrival of the fish at the table was greeted with suppressed laughter. The fish's back was blue-green and thickly covered with translucent scales. One chef skillfully slid a knife from tail to head, stripping away the scales. There was a burst of applause. The eyes had already been removed. The open mouth had no tongue in it. The chef rapidly cut up the body and divided it among eleven plates. Finally, only the eyeless fish-head and backbone remained. "Now then, ladies and gentlemen, let us raise our glasses and make a toast. To the future." Over the skeleton of the fish, glasses clinked. To the future.

For a while, everyone forgot to talk and ate fish. One could hear only the sounds of metal against china, and quick intakes of air between bites.

It was a relief to me that everyone was eating. When they eat, they don't talk.

I'm not well suited to the task of interpreting to begin with. I hate talking more than anything, especially speaking my mother tongue.

Until I started elementary school, I called myself by my

name. When school began, the teachers told the girls to call themselves *watashi* and the boys to say *boku*. At first everyone was embarrassed and mumbled compromises like *atai* and *boku-chan*, but soon, at least in class, everyone was using the words *watashi* and *boku* quite properly. I was the only one who couldn't, and since I didn't want anyone to find out, I stopped talking. I spoke only to my mother. I called myself exactly what my mother called me. Soon I went to middle school, where I was no longer able to avoid speaking, so I stuttered: *Wa,wa,wa,ta,ta,ta,shi...* The *Watashi* fell to pieces with extra vowels between its spaces: that was the name for myself which I finally arrived at. When I stuttered, all the extra vowels made it feel like singing, and it felt good to speak that way.

I heard the click of a cigarette lighter. Evidently someone had begun to smoke. The faces around me were flushed from the wine. When jaw muscles relax, the atmosphere becomes relaxed as well. People's mouths fell open like trash bags, and garbage spilled out. I had to chew the garbage, swallow it, and spit it back out in different words. Some of the words stank of nicotine. Some smelled like hair tonic. The conversation became animated. Everyone began to talk, using my mouth. Their words bolted into my stomach and then back out again, footsteps resounding up to my brain. The chunk of fish in my stomach was having a bad time of it and began to protest. My stomach muscles clenched up and I began to stutter. It felt good to stutter. "Tha, tha, tha, that," I said. The skin of my stomach grew taut like a bagpipe and I bellowed, "That ha, ha, ha, has, has." I didn't know myself whether I was laughing or stuttering, but it felt agreeable. The words scattered and rose fluttering into the air.

The others noticed the change in me and fell silent.

"Are you all right?" the woman opposite me whispered, glancing over at the company president.

"Excuse me, please." I stood up and went to look for the bathroom. The restaurant's long hallway continued into the hotel, and I found myself lost in its back corridors. There was no one else in sight. I saw only rows of doors. Finally I saw a door with the silhouette of a lady on it. I went in, pressed myself against the heater by the window, and slumped down. The scale whose pans were trembling inside my ear suddenly pitched to one side, and I found myself falling down a bottomless pit.

4

From far away came a crackling sound. I wanted to open my eyes, but from the inside I couldn't tell where my eyelids might be. From behind the network of my capillary vessels, I was trying to remember a face.

My mouth was dry, like a scab, and my tongue stuck to my palate. I could breathe only through my nose. The smell of milk boiling. There was a lot of sugar in the milk. The smell of sugar burning. Saliva gradually collected in my mouth. My tongue grew moist and I could move it again. Something wet and soft was touching my lips from the outside. The sole came slipping into my mouth and played with my tongue, gently at first, then with more force. Finally the sole gripped my tongue between its teeth and ate it up.

At that moment my surroundings grew bright. By my head sat an unfamiliar woman who was wiping my forehead with a wet towel. The right side of the woman's face was distorted by burn scars like hardened lava. The left side had a thoughtful expression I found beautiful. This was unmistakably the beauty of a woman of forty, but every time I blinked she looked different, now like a girl and now an old woman. She wore the sky-blue uniform of the hotel staff. On the blank wall behind the woman hung a torn employee roster. I seemed to be in a room for the hotel staff. When the cold towel touched my forehead, a delicious feeling of strength began to rise along my spine like mercury.

"How do you feel? A little better? You were lying on the bathroom floor. What happened to you?" The woman fixed her gaze on my face. Her eyes reminded me of blue gas flames.

After a little while she said, "Oh, of course. She doesn't understand." She took off her uniform, preparing to go home. I didn't want to be left alone, so I tried to ask her to take me with her, wherever she was going, but I couldn't find my vocal chords. When I sat up, my body had become very heavy.

After she changed her shoes, the woman said, "Well, let's go then. It's not very comfortable here, so let's go home."

We made our way toward the back entrance of the hotel. The woman stood in front of the punch clock, looking for her card. Apparently she couldn't find it, and after a while she gave up and shrugged. If she had had a card, I would have learned her name, I thought. Since she had no card, perhaps she was only pretending to be a hotel employee.

It was already dark outside. I wondered how many hours had passed. Although the woman had decided I didn't understand her, she continued to talk. "Some people say they don't like cleaning bathrooms, but I must say, for me it's the most interesting part of the day's work. Sweeping the lobby isn't nearly so good. Most of the customers' rectums aren't on straight, you can't imagine in what directions all the excrement flies. That comes from sitting in an office all day long. I used to work in an office myself, so I know what I'm talking about."

When I heard the word "office," I became sad. I wouldn't be able to go back to the office again. After all, I had disappeared on the job.

"It's certainly true that you don't see what goes on inside a person. Highly respectable gentlemen may produce the most miserable excrement, and perfectly proper executive secretaries may defecate all over the place. And of course they're all busy, I suppose, so they forget to flush."

We stopped at the red light and the woman took my arm. Several people were standing on the other side of the crosswalk, but none of them were looking at us. Even when no one is staring openly I tend to feel I'm being glanced at now and then, but today there was not even that. I felt invisible.

The woman's place was not far from the hotel. It was a basement apartment in an old gray building whose windows had iron bars like a prison.

The woman went down the pitch-black stairway in front of me, saying, "The light isn't working, so be careful where you step." The door wasn't locked. From inside came a smell that seemed familiar, but at first I couldn't place it. The woman groped for matches and lit a candle. The outlines of a chair and a table appeared against the darkness. It was somewhat lighter outside, and now and then we could see a pair of shoes pass by. The ceiling was low. I looked into the next room and saw a narrow bed. Something moved on the table. It was a black rat and had exactly the same face as the one I'd kept as a child.

"It's called Bear, that rat," the woman said. That had been the name of my rat, too—in Japanese, *Kuma*. The familiar smell was from the rat. The woman took several candles out of a drawer and lit them. With each new candle, the number of my shadows increased by one. Finally several shadows, dark ones and light ones, lay flickering in layers. I looked at the floor. The woman cast no shadow.

She put her hand on my shoulder and asked, "What would you like to drink?" Then for the first time she smiled. "Oh, of course, you can't talk." She had gone from saying, "you don't understand," to "you can't talk." It seemed I was now mute. The woman poured red wine into a glass and handed it to me. I had never seen so red a wine before: it was the color of blood. "Go ahead and start without me. I'm going to take a shower first." She took off her clothes. The scars on her face extended all the way down her back. They say that if over a third of your skin is burned, you will die, but this woman's burns appeared to cover far more than a third of her body. Only her breasts were pure white and reminded me of an infant's buttocks. The woman brought over a large washtub, climbed into it, and gingerly poured cold water from a pitcher over her shoulders. The water trickled down her breasts to her stomach, divided at her legs, and came together again at the bottom of the tub. The water dripping from her pubic hair played the xylophone. I was shivering with cold. The woman filled the pitcher again and repeated the process, but it looked less like a shower than a snake shedding its skin. The water slipped off her body like a transparent skin. "Unless I do this, I can't forget the bad things. Instead of screaming out loud, I freeze the screams and rinse them from my skin."

When the tub was full of water, the woman wrapped herself in a robe without first drying herself off or putting on underthings. She took a piece of cheese out of the refrigerator and placed it on the table. Suddenly rats came scurrying from all corners of the room. I couldn't tell which were rats and which were shadows.

"Come, little ones, aren't you hungry?" The woman cut the cheese into cubes and fed them to the rats. The rats took the cheese with their pink front paws and, silently gnawing, devoured it. When they had had enough, they wiped their mouths with their paws and groomed the fur on their backs. The woman sliced bread for me and held it out wordlessly. The bread was dry as coal. The woman didn't eat anything herself. "I don't need to eat any more," she said.

I gazed at her, trying to understand, but the burnt half of her face, the other half, and the third face made of bone beneath her skin gave me the impression I was sitting across from three different people. I began to feel dizzy.

"I don't know how many months it's been since I last sat down to a meal with anyone. I don't like people, usually," she said. She cut another slice of bread and held it out to me. I took it and ate it too, but it was like eating ash and my hunger remained. The room was cold.

She placed her palms on mine. "You live alone too, don't you? Living alone isn't a bit lonely. But you can't go around telling people that. You'd be killed in a minute. Not that there are many things you can safely go around saying. They're all deeply envious, you know."

From far off came the sounds of someone practicing the saxophone, not very well.

"So at some point I just stopped talking. That was why I gave up my job at the office. You can't very well not talk in an office. At the hotel I could work perfectly well without saying a word, but for some reason once I stopped talking, the most terrifying things started to leap into my eyes. You should be careful of your eyes, too."

In each of the woman's eyes reflected the flame of a candle. The flames wavered and swam out of her eyes like red tropical fish and began to dance about her ears. When I looked carefully, I saw that they were not flames but earrings in the shape of red tropical fish.

When the tropical fish glittered, they were reflected in the skin of her face and divided into drops of light. One of the fish slid down her shoulder and began to run about on the table. I screamed soundlessly. But it was only a rat that had stolen the earring and was running away with the earring held between its jaws. Dragged along by the rat, the earring got caught on a candlestick and knocked it over. Then one by one the candles fell over. The woman didn't move. The room grew as dark as if a curtain had fallen. I groped around for a candle. Night had fallen, and outside the window the streets were silent.

"Are you afraid of the dark?" I heard the woman say. "If you aren't afraid, leave it dark."

Now that I'd gotten used to not speaking, it was easy to get used to blindness as well. Only, perhaps because the flames had gone out, it was much colder now.

"Are you cold? The landlord turned off the heat a month ago. I don't get cold any more so it doesn't matter, but if you are, you'd better get into my bed. We can talk there."

She stood up, gripped my shoulder, and propelled me toward her bedroom. It was so dark I couldn't even make out the shapes of things. The wool blanket she pulled over me when I'd gotten into bed smelled of mildew.

The woman's outline gradually appeared in the shape of a keyhole. There was a burnt smell. I felt I had to escape, but on the other hand I was warming up and becoming sleepy.

"It isn't true that you don't have to suffer any more when you're dead. Dead people long for human contact even more than when they were alive." She slipped her hand under the blanket and placed it on my breast. My body turned to stone.

"Now close your eyes," she said. I closed my eyes and saw a desert. I felt as if I'd been tied up and couldn't move.

"Stick out your tongue. Let me lick it."

The bed turned into a sled that was being pulled across the sand by black rats. The rats grew wings and became bats. Drawn by bats, the sled flew up into the sky. So this is what it feels like to die, I thought, and suddenly I was terrified and tried to scream, but a big hand covered my mouth. "Don't scream. You're mute, don't you remember."

I couldn't breathe and pushed the woman away. She simply collapsed to the floor, almost too easily. I sat up and looked down at her. I felt as strong as a five-year-old boy.

The woman said, "I don't want to be dead all alone." She threw herself on the floor and sobbed. When I heard her sobbing, the strength went out of my knees and my eyes burned as if hot pokers had been stuck into them. I got out of bed, knelt on the floor and stroked the woman's back. Her back was hard and cold like a turtle's shell, but when I stroked it, it gradually became soft and warm.

After a while she raised her head and said, "Go home now, for tonight. Come again tomorrow night, won't you? If you come tomorrow, I'll give this back to you." She showed me what she held in her hand. It was my tongue.

5

When I arrived home the light was on. I remembered that in the morning Xander had telephoned about coming tonight. Inside, the room was dense with smoke.

Xander sat on the sofa, smoking. "Does she know what time it is?"

I looked at the clock but its hands were missing. I washed my face with cold water to rinse off the makeup.

"So she's working this late these days."

I faced the mirror and opened my mouth wide. There was no tongue, only a dark cave continuing far back. Xander wasn't really a photographer at all, he was my German teacher. Several years ago, when I had just arrived in this city and didn't know the language, it was Xander who first taught me how to speak. Xander is a teacher at a private language school, and gives individual tutorials to beginners. The school's pedagogical method consists of giving no explanations in other languages. The student repeats everything the teacher says until she's memorized it. I still remember the first time I met Xander. He wore a pair of blue jeans with creases ironed into them and a shirt as white as paper, and in this respect looked no different from a high school student; but the neck, chin and cheeks that grew up out of his collar were covered with the skin of a world-weary middle-aged man.

"This is a book." This was the first thing Xander ever said to me. I repeated the sentence without knowing where one word ended and the next began. "This is a book."

By the time we had moved on to ballpoint pen and ashtray, I was already in love with Xander. At least that was how I felt. I can fall in love on the spot with someone who teaches me words. As I repeated Xander's words, I felt that my tongue was starting to belong to him. When Xander drew on his cigarette, I began to cough and my tongue burned. Xander gave names to things as if he were the Creator. From this day on, a book became *Buch* to me, and a window *Fenster*.

The second class, however, did not go so easily. My happiness, which consisted of repeating everything I heard, was destroyed all too soon.

When asked, "Are you Japanese?" I would answer, "Yes, you are Japanese." The trick in this game was to change "you" into "I," but I didn't yet realize it.

Xander laughed like a bursting balloon. I didn't laugh. I repeated all of Xander's words, but not his laugh.

That day we went into town to buy dolls. Xander bought me a Japanese doll made of silk, and I bought him a blond violinist marionette. Since then when we had a conversation we used ventriloquism to make the dolls talk. The dolls talked about us in the third person.

"Will Xander be able to meet his sweetheart tomorrow?" the violinist would ask, and the silk doll would answer, "Probably not. She does not wish to meet." It went along like that. Soon I came to understand the first and second person, but Xander and I always stayed on third person terms.

•

"Where has she been? He was worried," the violinist said, and hugged the silk doll. Xander had become skillful as a puppeteer, and could do this kind of thing with one hand without looking. In his other hand he held a cigarette.

"He was worried. He was afraid there might have been an accident." With nimble fingers, the violinist peeled off the silk doll's clothes. The silk, which was the color of cherry blossoms, flew up into the air and fell to the floor in layers, whereupon it became red as blood. When the last layer was gone, only the doll's head remained, since her body consisted only of her clothes.

Next the violinist removed his tuxedo jacket, his white shirt, and his pants. He had no sex organ, just two spindly legs. This is often the case with children's toys.

"I can sew one out of scraps of cloth. Isn't it strange for there not to be one? Or maybe it would be better to carve one out of wood," I said once. But Xander was annoyed and refused. He couldn't stand to hear such things spoken of lightly.

"Even without things like that, there are differences between men and women. Men are moved from above by strings, whereas women are moved directly from behind. Men are made of wood, and women are made of silk. Men can close their eyes, and women can't. These differences suffice to produce love." Since Xander was of such an opinion, the violinist's body remained untouched.

"She hasn't turned mute now, has she?" the violinist

asked, worried. "She hasn't forgotten the language he taught her?" He was trembling and his joints clicked like castanets. For a long time now we'd been living like this, forgetting the obvious fact that dolls can't talk.

The violinist said, "They should go to sleep now. Probably tomorrow everything will look different." Xander ducked under the covers of the bed. At that moment the darkness was rent in two by the ringing of the telephone. It must be that woman. Xander sat up and reached for the receiver. I grabbed his arm and stopped him. Xander lay down again.

"Perhaps she has a new lover," the violinist murmured. The phone rang seven times and then stopped. I remembered that my mother always put down the receiver after seven rings. My mother might be ill. It was eleven o'clock in Japan. I wondered if I should call her. But without a tongue?

When I heard Xander begin to snore, I put a finger in my mouth. My tongue really was gone.

6

The next day was Sunday. I heard dishes clinking in the next room and opened my eyes. Apparently Xander was making coffee.

I looked in the mirror and found reflected there a healthy woman who looked just like the one in the photograph. Her cheeks glowed like peaches and her lips curved into a smile although I didn't particularly feel like smiling. I used makeup to create dark circles under my eyes. Then I filled in the contours of my lips with white lipstick, which made them look bloodless. Finally I rubbed the edges of my eyes with a little vinegar so that the skin shrank and puckered. Then I tore up the photograph and went into the kitchen where Xander was standing with his back to me, looking out the window.

Xander's name rang inside my skull but remained unspoken. I took milk out of the refrigerator and began to warm it. Xander turned around and put his hands on my shoulders, but when he saw the milk he quickly left the room. He couldn't stand the smell of warm milk.

The violinist and the silk doll were already sitting in their places at the doll's table, dressed in their Sunday best.

"Did something happen to her yesterday?" the violinist asked. He waited a long time for an answer, but finally gave up and said with a sigh, "It looks like she's stopped speaking the language he taught her."

I sliced bread. Xander didn't eat anything. The bread had just been baked, so it was moist and not very good. I wanted old, dry bread, as hard as coal.

"Will she take him where she went last night?"

I nodded. We walked along the empty Sunday morning

streets toward the hotel. From the hotel, I remembered the way very well: out the back door, across the street at the light, then down the first narrow alley on the right. The pavement and the façade of the old gray building were bathed in morning light and had nothing mysterious about them at all. From a distance I could already see the basement window.

There was no glass in the window frames, and the iron bars were covered with spider webs. I squatted down to look into the dim interior. Nothing but a few burnt black objects scattered about, and on the floor the outline of a person in chalk. The wall, too, was black and burnt.

"It was here?" Xander asked doubtfully. I nodded. An old woman came down the stairs and looked at the two of us with suspicion. "Are you looking for something?"

Xander gestured toward the basement apartment with his chin and asked, "What happened to this place?"

"Here? A month ago, a woman committed suicide, burnt herself to death, and it's just been left like that. They say they're investigating, there's suspicion of murder. It would be better just to clean up the place. Leave it like this and the rats multiply, and before you know it it's a nest for vagrants. Just last night I was sure I heard voices; it gave me a real fright. I live right upstairs, you see."

"What kind of person was she, the one who died?"

"A woman in her mid-forties. She lived alone and didn't talk much, we said hello now and then but never talked.

They say she worked in a hotel. I can't imagine it was murder."

"Why not?"

"Well, why would anyone want to kill her?"

"So it was suicide?"

"She lived alone, you know. Could be she was lonely."

"But it might have been an accident, don't you think? For instance she was smoking and her hair caught fire."

"Who knows, really? In any case a woman living alone, no good ever comes of that."

"And it was just a month ago, you say?"

"Yes, one month exactly."

When I rubbed my eyes on the way home, I found they were wet with tears. I looked at my reflection in a shop window. My eyes were red and swollen, and my face looked ravaged like a garden after a storm.

That night while Xander was asleep I went out again, alone, to the gray basement apartment. The night was heavy with fog. When I heard someone practicing scales on the saxophone in the distance, I began to run.

The basement windows were dimly lit. I rushed down the dark stairs and knocked on the door, which opened soundlessly. The woman came out and embraced me. I was still breathing hard, and my body swelled and shrank with each breath.

"You came! If you hadn't come, I'd have felt so lonely." The interior of the room was exactly as it had been the night before, and what I had seen in the morning seemed like a dream. On the table stood a single lit candle. The woman poured red wine into a glass. The wine smelled like blood. She cut me a slice of bread. This time, too, the bread was dry and tasted like coal. Today I found it delicious. Four black rats came to pick up the breadcrumbs.

"The fog is so dense, the town is like a jungle," said the woman, and stroked the back of my hand. On the patch of skin where she had stroked me, shining scales began to grow. The scales reflected the light in red and green. Even when the woman blew out the candle, the scales still sparkled.

"Now listen carefully. I'm speaking to you because you are the only one who understands my words." The woman's breath was as cold as a night wind on my cheek. "At first everyone will praise your scales and envy them, and you'll feel glad. But one day suddenly someone will say he's going to kill you. Suddenly they'll all hate you. Out of terror, your backbone will go soft, it will not hold itself erect. Your head will hang down in front. Then it's too late. They throw stones, there's a pounding in your head, and you realize the drum you hear is beating time for the sutras at your funeral."

The woman took my face in both hands. There was a sound like sparks flying up from a fire, and my scales began to grow. I touched them with my finger. They were rough and cold.

The woman thrust the five bony fingers of one hand into my hair. I heard the sounds of bats beating their wings, and my head became very heavy. I was overcome with weariness.

"Aren't you sleepy? Come to my bed. We'll sleep a little." The moment she said this, I heard the wooden door burst open. A dog was barking. Two large shadows threw themselves on me. I was knocked to the ground and cried out soundlessly.

"What are you doing here?" I heard men's voices. The room grew bright. I was lying in the middle of an empty burned-out room. The German shepherd smelled the wine on my lips, bared its teeth and growled. Behind the dog stood two men in uniform. The furniture had disappeared. So had the woman.

"Show me your papers," said a man with a beard exactly like a bush. I got to my feet. My clothing was streaked with soot.

"Your name?"

I tried to brush the soot from my clothes.

"I asked what your name is," Bush-beard snapped.

"I don't think she understands," said the other man, a beanpole. "Maybe she's ill. Look at her face, she looks like a ghost."

"Maybe she's a refugee."

"Anyway, she's not relevant to the case. Leave her alone."

Bush-beard tapped my back lightly three times with the stick he held in his hand and shouted, "Get out of here, go home! They find you in a place like this, they'll sell you." Beanpole gave a long piercing laugh like a siren.

7

"Now, begin from that corner." At some point, Bush-beard must have combed his bush and changed into a suit. I swung the heavy lead hammer and brought it down with a crash on the floor where Bush-beard was pointing. Rats scattered in all directions. The body of a rat that didn't manage to escape was smashed beneath the hammer. Beanpole wrote something in his notebook. Bush-beard pointed to another spot. I lifted the hammer and brought it down. I heard the rat's bones crack.

"A little more accurately please."

I wiped the sweat from my palms with a handkerchief.

"Please open the closet," the man said gently, so I opened it, and inside were a large number of rats huddled together trembling. When I raised the hammer, all the rats started running. The hammer fell. The last rat was too slow and gave a shrill squeal. Salty sweat trickled into them. I rubbed my eyes so I could aim where the man was pointing.

"Hurry!"

I lifted the hammer, staggering under its weight.

"Harder!"

I took aim and methodically delivered blow after blow as if I were stamping documents. There were fewer and fewer rats. Beanpole seemed to be recording the number of dead rats.

"Look, there too," said the man, pointing with his chin. A few rats were gnawing at the door, apparently attempting to escape. With my last ounce of strength, I raised the hammer. Its handle was damp. The instant before the hammer hit the floor, one of the rats turned around. I recognized its face, that of the woman who had set herself on fire.

When I woke up, my palms and hair were dripping with sweat. As after a long journey, my hair smelled foreign and I wanted to wash the smell away, but a bathtub resembles a coffin so I washed my hair in the kitchen sink. I filled the sink, dipped my hair into the water, and swirled it around. Out came dead leaves, butterflies' wings, dead ants, and dried lizards' tails.

When I stood in front of the mirror, what I saw reflected was not myself but that woman, unmistakably. I turned the mirror to the wall and decided not to put on any makeup.

I made warm milk and covered my knees with a blanket

as if I were ill, opened the newspaper and read the help wanted section of the classifieds. After what had happened, I didn't think I would be able to get any more interpreting jobs, so I would have to find new employment. Since my visa stipulated that I was ineligible to receive unemployment benefits, I couldn't turn to the unemployment office either.

"Wanted: woman with scales." A local circus was hiring women with scales on their skin. It was a unique opportunity for me. I stroked my face with a fingertip to make sure my scales were firm and in their best condition. To show I had scales all over, I put on a thin sleeveless silk blouse and a miniskirt.

The circus had seven tents set up on an empty lot outside of town. It was close to noon, but everyone might have been asleep still, it was so quiet. At the entrance to each tent was a sign indicating its function, such as "Department of Accounting" and "Wild Animals Division." I checked them one by one and finally reached a tent marked "Office of Human Resources."

Inside sat a man with a necktie and a piercing gaze.

I was about to say that I had come in response to the advertisement, then remembered that I had no tongue. The man grinned and said, "You must be the person with scales. We didn't expect to find one so soon. Last week our mermaid died of breast cancer and we've been at a loss."

The man seemed to have taken an immediate liking to me. "It's not good to touch a mermaid's breasts all the time.

And this friend of mine, a poet, insisted on drinking her milk every day, until finally she died."

He stood up and said, "Let me show you the sideshow." I remembered the sad snakes and salamanders I had seen in freak shows during my childhood. So this town, too, had such sad installations.

It was dark inside the tent and I couldn't see much. There was an eerie sound a bit like rustling grass. When the man turned on the light, at least ten women in miniskirts came into view, sitting at office desks and sorting papers. When the women saw the man, they shouted in unison, "Good morning!" They were all beauties who might have just stepped out of the pages of a fashion magazine, and their cheeks and lips were as red as if they'd just been slapped.

"This is the pride of our circus, our freak show." There were neither snakes nor salamanders, but this was clearly it. I had no idea why they needed a person with scales in this office. The women looked at me and smiled, but said nothing.

After the man left the room, the women wordlessly began to slap each other. For some reason I alone was not slapped. There were a lot of small holes in the walls. Perhaps people were watching from outside. When one of the women fell to the floor gasping for breath, the whole group threw themselves on her and dressed her in a wedding gown. This procedure was repeated with a second woman, and in the end the place was full of brides lying on the ground. Terrified, I climbed up a pole and sat on a trapeze.

"Get down from there!" I heard drunken men shouting from outside. There had been spectators after all. "You can't run away from life! Get down!"

Then someone cut the rope supporting the trapeze. I tumbled headlong to the ground and lost consciousness.

When I came to, the mass wedding was in full swing, and I was lying on a fish platter in the middle of the table. The brides had resigned from their jobs and washed off their makeup, and the bridegrooms looked exhausted. One of the women stood up, raised her glass and announced, "From now on we intend to lead honest lives!" "Honest lives!" echoed the other women. "If things stink we'll say they stink! People with scales stink!" The men, looking terribly exhausted, sat in their chairs waiting for the ceremony to end. "If we want something, we'll say we want it! We want money!" the women shouted in unison. Glasses clinked. "A toast to freedom!"

The chef arrived with a large knife in his hand. When he took a bow, everyone present burst into applause. He placed the blade of the knife against my back and stripped off my scales. The scales flew into the air like cherry blossom petals, and my skin burned. There was a roar of applause like waves breaking.

•

When I woke up, I was lying with my fingers under me. They were cold and numb. I always feel relieved when I wake up from a dream. No work is more exhausting than sleep.

Since the mirror was turned to the wall, I couldn't put on makeup. I warmed some milk, sat down on a kitchen chair and opened the newspaper. In the human interest section was a photograph of that woman. There were no burn marks on her face. A photographer must have retouched the picture to make her look so unhappy. As well as unattractive. The article said that although there had been an investigation due to the suspicion of foul play, the investigation was now closed and it was concluded that her death had been a suicide. Apparently it was standard practice to retouch the photo of a suicide to make her look unattractive.

8

The mirror that was hanging with its face to the wall beside my photograph had been a parting gift from my mother.

The month before, I had traveled to Japan for the first time in years. My mother hadn't come to meet me at the airport. She always said the sound of airplanes reminded her of the Tokyo air raids, and so the airport was the one place she couldn't bring herself to set foot in. In those air raids she had lost her entire family.

It was a strange homecoming. When at last I reached home and knocked on the door, my head full of impossible memories, there was no answer. Quietly I tried the door. It wasn't locked. Inside it was completely dark. I turned on the light and opened the sliding door. A machine that looked like a cross between a bicycle and a handloom filled the small room entirely. Behind it, on a futon, lay my mother. She pulled herself up, gazing into space like a blind woman.

"*Okaasan, watashi yo.*"

I hadn't spoken Japanese in a long time. In the word *okaasan* (mother) I met my old self, and when I said *watashi* (I) I felt as though I were my own simultaneous interpreter.

My mother looked at my face, but her expression did not change. It was as if she didn't know who I was. Then she stood up slowly, thought for a little while, and said, "Oh, it's you." Then two tears the size of marbles rolled down from her eyes, but her face remained expressionless. An image from a European movie passed through my mind: a mother and daughter throwing their arms around each other in ecstatic reunion.

My mother's face was covered with luminous scales.

"You look well—as if you've gotten younger," I said. She pointed to the strange machine and said, "It's because of the daily training." She rolled up her sleeve and showed me her muscular arm. "But I've developed more than just muscles. I have a hysterical lump in my throat that hurts and makes it hard to breathe."

I didn't know what a hysterical lump was, but I didn't have the courage to ask.

"And you, why has your hair gotten so thin?" Alarmed, I touched my hair.

"And why does it have such a reddish gleam?"

"It must be the light."

"Why the light?"

"The light's different here, so my hair looks different."

"Is that so," my mother said, looking sadly at my hair.

"What is that machine?" I asked.

"It's a training machine for body-building."

"Why did you get a thing like that?"

"I don't have anything else to do. Besides, it would be terrible if for instance I fell ill and stood in the way of your career. I decided I ought to strengthen myself a little."

"But you're fine, you're already healthy."

"I'm not in the least healthy. I read in a magazine that when new muscle tissue forms, the amount of female hormones in the body decreases, which results in a reduced rate of depression, but that's a lie. It just gets harder to breathe, because of the hysterical lump. Besides, I have the feeling that without you here I'm gradually forgetting all my words."

My mother glanced me up and down.

"How did you get such an Asian face?"

"What are you talking about, Mother? I am Asian."

"That's not what I meant. You've started to have one of those faces like Japanese people in American movies."

I looked around the room. There were no mirrors. That was why my mother hadn't noticed her own scales.

"What do you use my room for now?"

Instead of answering, my mother asked, "Why don't you cut your hair? They say the god of death can grab hold of long hair."

I was eager to see my old room again.

When I opened the door to my old, beloved room, there was a smell of mildew. The window was gone. On the floor, stuffed animals were lying in their own entrails, like corpses on a battlefield. Several wooden boxes were stacked up along the wall. I opened them and found diapers. Underneath were bibs. All were moldy.

"What's this?"

"Your old baby clothes."

"Why don't you throw them away? They're full of scales—I mean, mold."

My mother had never thrown anything away. She always used to say a person who had grown up in the war years could never bring herself to throw something out.

She picked up a bib and stroked it as if it were a precious thing. "You were still breastfeeding at the age of five. Even in front of guests you would ask for milk and cry; I didn't know what to do."

I had no memory of my mother's breast. I wondered when I had last touched her.

"I spoke to a doctor, and he laughed and told you, 'That's not what girls are supposed to want.' Then, I don't know what you were thinking, but you took the china toy you were holding and threw it in his face as hard as you could. You injured him, and he was so angry he scowled like the prince of hell and shouted, 'I'll pull your tongue out!'"

I didn't remember any of this.

In the corner of the room stood a rusty birdcage with some thin white bones lying scattered inside. That must have been my pet rat that had died ten years earlier.

"Those are Kuma's bones. You remember, your pet rat?" my mother said gaily.

"Why don't you just throw them out?"

"But what if she came back?"

"Who's going to come back? I'm never coming back again, that's certain."

"But my daughter might still come back. She's pursuing her career, and then she'll come back."

"I'm not coming back, ever. Even if I came back, I would be somebody else already."

"Who are you?"

"What are you talking about? It's me."

"How can you say that, how can you throw words around like that?" She suddenly squatted down and began to cry.

"But what else am I supposed to call myself?"

"Oh, when did you start speaking like this." My mother continued to cry. She sounded like a broken flute.

"Mother, stop thinking about the past. Let's be practical and think about the future."

"What future? When is that?"

"You should stop crying, it makes you grow scales."

"I have nothing to wait for but death. You have a job, you have friends, but I threw away everything to bring you up." My mother seemed to have shrunk, about to drown in her clothes.

"Mother, I don't have a job."

"But you always wrote so much about work in your letters."

"I made it all up. You talk about my career, but it's all I can do to earn enough for food."

"You don't need a career, it's all right. Why do you want to go on living in a place like that? Come back home. Don't go back there!"

Just then a fly appeared. My mother took aim with a fly swatter and smashed it against the wall. My mother hates everything that flies through the air.

"Oh, it's time for my training," she said, glancing at the clock. The clock had no hands. She sat down at the bicycle-loom and began to pedal. The pedals caused chains to move, the chains moved cogs, these moved other cogs, and soon a mechanical-sounding music began to play. The strange thing was that none of the notes had pitch or length, they were simply born in the distance like a desert whirlwind, they wrapped themselves around me and sucked me in. I began to spin round and round. I felt drunk and sick to my stomach as if after a wild celebration, but when I tried to vomit, nothing came up but laughter. It was so much fun I couldn't help it. With every revolution, I became one year younger. There was no longer any front or back, and I couldn't see. My knees grew soft, my heels grew soft, I could no longer stand. My lips and anus grew hot. I was crying like an infant, the shrieks of a dying child being sucked into its mother's vagina. Howling, I vanished into the dark hole of the whirlwind. With the last of my strength, I cursed my mother: "Death to the women with scales!"

Suddenly my body was covered with scales and I fell into my own vagina, the dark hole of the whirlwind.

9

I wasn't really an interpreter. Sometimes I pretended to be one, but really I was just a typist. Now that I had lost my tongue, I could no longer even pretend to interpret. My work was limited to hammering out words whose meanings escaped me. After half a day's typing, my back felt like a turtle's shell. By afternoon, my neck wouldn't turn, and by evening my fingers were cold. Still I went on striking the keys of the cheap mechanical typewriter. When I struck the keys, the arms of the letters flew up like the arms of drowning people. By midnight I was unable to see. Still I went on blindly. I kept receiving more and more assignments since typists who translate the voices of ghosts into written words have become a rare commodity. Of course I had no time for sleep. Sometimes I fell asleep with my head on my typewriter. When I woke up I would continue.

One could say I had given the woman my life along with my tongue. Every evening I listened for her voice and wrote down her words. So of course I couldn't understand anything Xander was saying. Indeed, I couldn't remember whether I'd ever understood the things he said.

Xander wasn't really a German teacher, he was a carpenter. Anything that could be made of wood he would make for me. The desk and the chair I could never get up from were made by Xander. To keep me from falling out of the chair when I fell asleep, Xander attached my heels to its legs with thick nails.

My energy, though, was nearing its limits. My eyeballs

shrank with exhaustion, and the sound of my pounding heart echoed painfully within my skull. When I had to vomit, a greenish fluid came up from my empty stomach. Xander felt sorry for me and made me a bed.

The bed was a wooden box just my length with a lid that shut. Once the lid was on, it was pitch black inside and I couldn't see a thing. I couldn't hear anything, either. So no one would disturb me as I slept, Xander fastened the lid with nails.

My wooden box was a four-legged bird covered with scales that was called Sarcophagus. With me inside, this bird began to run about clumsily, as if its feet were stuttering, and once its speed increased, the bird's body became hot and hard, and finally it raised its hook-shaped neck and took off into the sky.

Looking down at the earth from above, we headed for the realm of the dead.

Seven-tenths of the globe is covered with water, so it isn't surprising that one sees different patterns on its surface every day. Subterranean water shapes the earth's surface from below, the ocean's waves eat away at the coastline, and human beings blast holes in mountainsides, plow the valleys for fields and fill in the ocean with land. Thus the shape of the earth is constantly changing.

I spread out a map of the world. On the map, the water

has suspended any motion, so all the cities look as if they're always in exactly the same place. Countless red lines, perhaps air routes or fishnets, run from city to city. The earth's face is caught in this net. Every day, human beings adjust the face with makeup, using the map as their model.

Like a herd of frightened sheep, the clouds hurriedly withdraw. In the distance, many fighter planes can be seen, bombs falling from their anuses.

Finally the clouds vanish entirely and the world becomes visible below. It is a sea of fire.

"Coffee or tea?" A ghost stewardess flies up to me, holding two pitchers. The distinction means nothing to me since I have no tongue. The stewardess is carrying a baby on her back. The baby is hungry and crying for milk. I also want milk, not tea or coffee. Xander's voice says, "The smell of warm milk makes me sick to my stomach." At this moment, milk as white as paper begins to flow out of the stewardess's pitchers; it puts out the battle fires that have engulfed the planet, mixes with the ash, soaks into the earth and disappears. When all the fires have been extinguished, no milk is left. I hear the woman's voice saying, "I never once got any milk." She was born the year World War II came to an end.

Finally we leave the ruins behind us and the desert's wrinkles begin.

"Meat or vegetarian?" asks a second ghost stewardess. It makes no difference if I eat the skeletons of grasses or the corpses of quadrupeds. After a war, everything you eat tastes of ash.

In the desert someone builds a factory in which the woman, now dressed in work clothes, has sex with a handsome man. Behind him, an even more handsome man is waiting his turn. And behind him stands a man twice as handsome as the last, and so on, all of them in a long, long line. But when the five o'clock bell rings, the woman takes off her work clothes and rushes home.

The sun flees behind the globe. In the darkness, my scale-covered bird increases its speed. On the earth below, the light of a candle can be seen. When all the inhabitants of the city have fallen asleep, a single person, the woman, sits awake. One by one the hairs on her head turn into writing brushes and begin composing letters. The envelopes bear no addresses. I try reading the letters with my telescope, but the moment each one is finished, a policeman wearing pajamas comes in to take it away. Not for purposes of censorship. This country has no such laws. There is no paper in the bathrooms, so everyone uses letters instead. And afterwards they are illegible. Every time a policeman comes out of the bathroom, he gives a yawn and shoots at the woman with his pistol as if activating the shutter of a camera. More and more holes appear in the woman's head, but she never falls down. She appears to be a mechanical writing doll.

"Is it you?" Deep within my ear I hear Xander's calm

voice. The woman's voice answers for me, shouting, "Yes, it's you," and then she chokes with laughter. Apparently Xander can't hear her.

Xander's voice grows hard. "You've stopped speaking the language I taught you, haven't you?" The woman laughs herself into a coughing fit.

"You kissed a dead person."

The woman continues to laugh. I start to cry, but of course neither voice nor tears come.

"You gave a dead person your tongue."

All at once I realize that the scale-covered bird called Sarcophagus is, in fact, the woman. I push open the lid and climb out.

Sky and earth have come to an end, and before me lie desolate grasslands full of slender blades swaying in the air. I remember having felt this way when I first left my mother's womb.

With all my strength, I embrace the cold body of the scaly bird. In my arms, each of its scales becomes a wind chime that rings. Sharp, gentle, bitter, soft notes penetrate my bones, and now my bones, too, begin to ring. This ringing gradually gives rise to a strength which belongs to no one.

Then Xander catches up to me on his motorcycle and knocks me over. I fall backward and hit the back of my head on the asphalt of the highway.

"You think everything's fine as long as you're all right? Don't you care about rescuing her? What that woman needs is an umbrella and love."

A gray rain mixed with factory smoke begins to fall. The scale-covered bird screams in pain. I open my umbrella above its head. The rain soaks my hair and makes the hair so heavy it tears at the roots and pulls them out. It wasn't the light that made my hair so thin, it was the rain.

"This is a nude bathing establishment, so please remove all scales," a supervisor admonishes through a megaphone. I see a large number of naked men and woman bathing in the gray rain and stretching out in the middle of the highway. Only the heretic women sit wrapped in shawls at the edge of the road.

Xander places a heavy kitchen knife in my hand and says, "Strip off their armor, make them naked and free so they can love life."

I concentrate as if taking an exam, trying to understand Xander's words.

"You ought to be able to understand the word for love as easily as you understand the word for umbrella. Only barbarians don't understand it."

I nod and strike at the scales with the knife. At once the wind chimes fall silent and tumble to the road—shriveled, blood-smeared plums.

The scaly bird is dead, but the knife can find no peace,

it dances wildly through the air and stabs my right eye. The eyeball's surface bursts like the skin of a plum, and a soft red substance, a surprising amount of it, comes streaming out.

10

Only adolescent girls are unable to put on makeup without a mirror. Adult women can do without. The location of the skin can be determined by touch. You just put out your hand and feel where this world ends: that's where my skin is. The skin is a membrane separating this world from the other one. I apply a special makeup until my skin becomes transparent. Of course it isn't enough to rub the creme into the skin of one's face, since when the face becomes invisible, the body appears to have been beheaded. So I'm careful not to miss a single spot.

When my skin has finally become transparent, the figure of the dead woman appears behind it.

I always put on makeup before going to bed.

Since I never leave the house, I get puzzled questions: "Don't you have a sweetheart?"

But I have no time to go out because I sleep so much.

Every evening, the woman visits this world through my skin. I can't see her because the lamp is broken and the room is dark. I can't hear her either. I can only feel my bones become a conduit for her trembling. Then I hold my breath and concentrate on this vibrato of bones. It is a sound that cannot be transformed into music, an oscillation that can never become a note.

By morning, the woman is gone. I remain lying in bed a long while. By the time the reverberations have died down and I start to wonder if I shouldn't get up, it's already dark out. I get into the bathtub, carefully put on makeup and then go back to bed.

"What do you do for a living?"

The first thing everyone always wants to know is what I do when I'm not sleeping, what sorts of exams and theses I have to my name as if they wanted to reserve a place in my curriculum vitae for the date of my death. There ought to be a curriculum vitae whose first line is the date of death.

Since I have no tongue, I cannot be an interpreter, cannot translate what the woman says into words that can be easily understood. Since I have forgotten the letters of the alphabet, I can no longer be a typist either. The letters all look the same to me, like rusty nails twisted into shapes. For this reason, I can no longer even copy down poems written by others. And of course I am farthest of all from being a model, since in photographs I am completely invisible.

I am a transparent coffin.

II. WHERE EUROPE BEGINS

THE REFLECTION

Once upon a time there was a monk who saw the reflection of a monk in a pond and leapt into the water to embrace it. The pond lay at the edge of a small forest. The temple lay at the other end of the forest. A narrow path led from the temple through the forest to the pond. There was also a second path that led from the temple to a village. This path was seldom used. The monk arose each morning at five, cleaned the rooms of the temple, studied the sacred texts and spent his afternoons working in the garden. There he planted vegetables and grain, which sustained him. In the evenings he continued his studies of the sacred texts. When he stayed awake too long, it sometimes happened that he fell asleep still seated at his desk.

The moon was full. The monk fell asleep reading a prayer book. Fast asleep, he walked through the forest to the pond.

The monk walks along the edge of the pond and sees
the moon in the water.
He sees it with closed eyes, for he is asleep.
Seeing it does not cause him to awaken.
Awakening would not help him to see.
He leaps into the water.
And?
He drowns.
He drinks.
He drinks the water. He drinks the moon.
He wanted to embrace the moon. But now he's
drunk it.
And he drowns.
Who are you?
I like to read, and I take walks at night when I
can't fall asleep. I always see exactly
what I've just read.
You see what you've read in the water.
You see it in the sky.
The monk doesn't just leap into the water straight off.
He glances to the right and left.
He glances up and notices there is no moon in the sky.

I beg your pardon?
The moon as such does not exist. There is only its
    reflection in the water.
Perhaps you just can't see it.
Seeing doesn't mean much.
Perhaps the moon is just missing today.
It's never been there.
Then why does the monk see the moon's reflection in
    the water?
The reflection is from yesterday.
Or the moon is from yesterday.
You can't see yesterday's moon.
The moon no one sees belongs to yesterday.
It's in the wrong time.
You can't help but see wrong what
    lives in the wrong time.
The monk sees with the wrong gaze.
No, the moon just appears at the wrong moment.
Even a right moon can be wrong
    at the wrong moment.
The moon no one sees is a wrong moon.
Something no one sees can't be wrong.
The monk doesn't even notice he's seeing
    a wrong moon.
The moon doesn't know it's being seen
    as a wrong moon.
It's only a reflection.

A reflection is never wrong.
It's not a reflection, it's a water moon.
The monk sees a moon made of water.
This moon is fluid. It is not superficial.
It is only superficial when seen.
It is no longer superficial when touched.
The hand that has touched it is wet.

One day later the newspaper reported the monk's suicide. Many in the village were surprised, since it was rare for a monk to die in this way. Only now did they realize how little they knew about his life. They had seldom seen him. When they conversed with him, he spoke only of death. But this was only because of his profession. It didn't occur to any of them that the monk, too, would one day die. Some said that he had probably fallen into the pond and drowned by accident. Others said this was impossible, as the monk was an excellent swimmer. When he was still a small child, he liked to swim in the pond as much as all the other village children. After becoming a monk he stayed out of the water, for he had come to revere it.

The monk leaps into liquid, to embrace liquid.
He does not drown. He clings to the water moon.
    His hands are wet.
For a dissolving gaze there is nothing more solid than
    water. For water there is nothing more solid

than a human gaze.
The monk gazes upon the water with closed eyes.
He does not swim. He sits upon water.
He lies down on water. He does not know where the
sky is, where the earth.
He who can forget the sky does not sink.
Who are you.
I talk too much and write too little.
He who sits near the water speaks a great deal.
The water supports all conversations.
He who lies upon the water has ceased to speak.
Who are you?
I swim too often and speak too seldom.

A girl from the village walked to the pond. Her mother had told her the monk had died there. It was a quiet afternoon. The sky grew darker and darker, the air cooler. Then a wind sprang up and unsettled the water's surface. The girl heard a sound from beneath the water.

What do you hear now?
I hear a water sound.
Every water sound casts some light.
Let there be light! And there was sound.
It is bright.
Can you see more now?
No, it is too loud here. That's why you can hardly see.

In sleep, one sees only by hearing.
What do you see now?
I hear a water sound.
In the nocturnal landscape the monk washes his hands.
Because his hands are too clean. He rinses away their
cleanness.
He washes his hands with the wind.
And the wind has the form of a wave.
The wave reaches the monk, and he is wet.
The monk does not unclothe.
He never shows himself naked.
In his robe he sits upon the water.
The folds of his robe become waves.

One newspaper article said the monk had been found naked. The corpse was floating on the water when a fisherman came to gather insects.

The girl wanted to find the dead monk's robe. If it was true he had been found naked, his robe had to be somewhere near the pond. After a while it grew dark. The mother was waiting at home for the girl. She thought the girl had gone to the next village to visit her old teacher. The girl looked for the robe and couldn't find it. Disappointed, she sat down and gazed into the water. Something gleamed: it was a book.

The monk never unclothes.
He never parts from his robe.
He parts only from his prayer book.
He throws the book into the pond.
And it sinks into the water.
The water is cold.
But the book does not drown. The texts can breathe
without air.
The book lies underwater.
The monk has nothing left to read. He has time now
to drown.
Anyone can swim. But only he who knows that the
water has no form can drown. Only he who
knows that his body has no form can drown.
Only he who reads can drown. That water and body
are formless can be found only in the book.
The book lies in the water.
It glows as the sky darkens.
From outside the water the book cannot be read.
The monk leaps into the water to read the book.
And he drowns.
He sinks beneath the water and sees not a splinter of
the moon.
He sees the splinters of the reflection.
When the monk leaps into the water the image on its
surface shatters.

The girl squatted down, stretched out her arms toward the book and tried to reach it. The soil beneath her feet was soft and subsided, and the water was much deeper than it had appeared. The girl fell into the cold water and drowned. That night there was no moon.

The moon sees the monk in the water, reading the
    prayer book.
The moon leaps into the water to embrace the monk.
It shatters.
It splinters.
The splinters scatter through the water.
The pond now is empty.
In the empty pond lies a book.
And a monk who is reading the book.
And the moon which is embracing the monk.
And a girl who is dead.
Once upon a time.
You are now. You are here.

SPORES

Kinoko-san says "disheard" instead of "misheard." At first I thought it just sounded that way because my eardrums have gotten loose, but no matter how many times I hear her say it, it really does sound like "disheard."

Sometimes I almost get up the nerve to correct her: "It's not 'disheard,' actually. One says 'misheard.'" But then I swallow my unspoken words.

Every morning at six, Kinoko-san arranges the neckline of her kimono just so, draws herself up straight and smiles with her shiny cheeks and kindly-looking crow's feet. Even when I'm absolutely certain about something, she can dismiss it with a bright laugh, saying, "I myself might think the same if I were just a bit younger."

When Kinoko-san laughs, I think of the word *aristocrat.* Willowy, pliant, the nape of her neck exposed, her cheeks soft. Aristocrats are crats who have been "arist." The moment this thought appeared, I realized I didn't know how to write it out. There are many ways to write a wrist.

I don't even know how to write "Kinoko", for that matter. Perhaps Kinoko-san herself doesn't know, or she has forgotten or wants to keep it hidden—in any case, she won't tell me. She did, though, tell me this much, that at first she didn't even realize the name Kinoko sounded just like the Japanese word for mushroom. Furthermore, it was originally her family name, and the "–ko" was simply part of it, but when written phonetically, the "–ko" looks like the kind of ending which used to be tacked on to the end of girls' names. So people are always assuming Kinoko is her given name and calling her "Kinoko-san" with an air of particular intimacy. Kinoko-san herself doesn't like to be constantly clearing up misconceptions, so she lets it go. I wish I had a *kanji* dictionary. Even if I could never leave the house again, even if I could never again have anything to call my own, if only I could just once consult a *kanji* dictionary! No doubt because of all this brooding, I had a strange dream. I was sitting alone in a big *zashiki* room with mats on the floor when a roof beam above me suddenly burst into flames. In a panic I opened the sliding paper doors and rushed into the hall, but then on the hall floor I found a *kanji* dictionary bound in leather. I tried to escape with it, but the cover was stuck to the floor and I couldn't pull it loose. The book was going to burn up along with the rest of the house so I tried to look up the most important characters, but when I started to count the number of strokes, smoke came pouring in from one of the rooms and I couldn't see. I tried to wave away the smoke with my hand, but then I started coughing, my hands were shaking, and I kept losing count. The fire seemed to be getting closer, my skin was hot, and the ends of my hair began to sizzle. Why was the dictionary stuck to the floor? I didn't need the cover—all I had to do was tear out the pages and take them with me. So I tried to pull out all the pages at once, and heard a shriek. Impossible, I thought, looking around. There was no one there. Perhaps certain books do scream when they're torn apart. My field of vision was washed in red from the flames. Crying, I woke up.

The Japanese word for "misheard" sounds like a frog croaking. If there is a frog that croaks "misheard," there must be others that croak "mistook," "misread," and so on. You could line them all up in a row.

When Kinoko-san addresses someone, for some reason she always starts by saying, "Lend me your ear." She says it so deliberately and with such earnestness one really feels one ought to cut off one's ear with a fruit knife and lend it to her. A chilling thought. If only she would say the words a bit more lightly, it wouldn't be necessary to take them so literally. She also likes to say, "I'll just borrow your ear now, if I may." Sometimes I want to tell her, "An ear isn't the sort of thing you just borrow from other people whenever you feel like it," but then I swallow hard and hold my peace. I bite my nails and tell myself, "All right, then. If she wants an ear, I'll give her an ear. An ear isn't something you have less of just because you lend it out. Let's say you slice it off with one slash of a razor—fine! Then just wind a bandage around what's left." My speech, unlike Kinoko-san's, is becoming less elegant by the day.

When approaching another person, it's immature to begin by saying, "Um..." or "Uh..." On the other hand, "You know" is a bit too self-important, "Excuse me" is too formal, "By the way" too inefficient, and "Now then" too brisk. When you consider the options, Kinoko-san's ear-borrowing isn't so bad after all. Having heard it so often, I'm getting used to the phrase. You can get used to almost any phrase if you hear it every day.

But now Kinoko-san has come up with more and more radical variants. First she changed the phrase to "Rend me your ear," then to "render" and even "surrender." Since she's been growing more elegant daily, it isn't surprising to hear her append an extra syllable, or shift the consonants in one direction or another. Still, it makes my chest clench up to think of rendering my ears.

This reminds me of a painting, an old oil painting about

the size of a window. An angel is blowing into a horn, and from the other end of the horn a spurt of liquid flies across the sky right into the Virgin Mary's ear. Just such a portrayal of the Annunciation is hanging in the abbot's room. It's certainly a bit risqué.

"Isn't this picture a bit risqué?" I ask warily, but the abbot only says, "Not at all, not at all."

Angels are urban creatures, and thus not necessarily dangerous, though apparently you're running quite a risk when you see a blue butterfly. The day I first heard this, I was out in the yard alone in the evening and saw a butterfly. Was it blue? I couldn't be sure it wasn't. Looking at it more carefully, I noticed that the butterfly had a tiny human face. It fluttered around my head until I couldn't tell where was earth and where was heaven. And then it happened. Before I knew what had hit me, there was a moist afterglow shimmering inside my head. Once that happens, there isn't much you can do. Still, I could have managed, but then I began to slide backwards, further and further. Perhaps behind me the sea was very low. No matter how far I slipped, I kept slipping more. Instead of screaming for help, I said, "Kinoko-san, courage! Don't give up." Kinoko-san gave me a surprised look. Somehow I was back in my room, which was strange.

Sometimes it's a relief to have Kinoko-san nearby, and other times her presence is oppressive. When Kinoko-san coughs, all sorts of strange thoughts run one after the other through my head. When at last they subside, Kinoko-san turns over in her sleep. Then I start to hear her voice saying urgently over and over, "Please, I want you to surrender your ears." I wish I could make her stop. What would make her stop? I get as far as deciding I could fit the palm of my hand exactly over Kinoko-san's mouth and hold it there to keep her voice in, and then I fall asleep.

Rather than trying to correct Kinoko-san's pronunciation of the word "misheard," I decided to insert all sorts of other expressions into her ear, things like "didn't quite catch that" and "thought I heard when actually she said" and "in one ear and out the other." Perhaps Kinoko-san would abandon her fixation on the one single expression and open her ears to others. This might be enough to make my murderous intentions, which have been provoked by the constant irritation of a single nerve, vanish in the wind.

"Kinoko-san, there's this woman who never says anything interesting, so whatever she says to me goes in one ear and out the other, but the other day I didn't hear what she said just when it was actually important, and now I'm regretting it. You remember that tall high school student who is always coming by, what was his name again? He mentioned his name but I didn't quite catch it, and the question is, is he her grandson or not? Apparently she doesn't have any children. Is it possible for a person to have grandchildren without having any children?" Kinoko-san gave me a sympathetic look and said smoothly, "Oh, certainly." At the time, a deep skepticism rose within me and I began to wonder whether Kinoko-san's sense of reason hadn't finally been warped, but when I thought it over the next day, I realized that one can indeed have grandchildren without first having children. Perhaps it was not Kinoko-san who was warped, but my own brain that was beginning to soften.

Sometimes Kinoko-san would wake up in the middle of the night and say, "Surrend me your ear." The odd thing is that I would wake up not from hearing her voice, but a few seconds before she began to speak. It's coming, I have a feeling it's coming, I know it's coming, I would think, holding my breath, and sure enough she'd say it. There was never anyone around to save me. All alone, I would lie grieving over the fate of the ear I would have to surrender. To add insult to injury, there wasn't anything in particular Kinoko-san wanted to say. Once she came out with "render me your ear now," she would just look at me without saying anything, the smell of disinfectant would rise in the darkness, everything so quiet we could hardly breathe. Distressed, I would seek out other topics, start talking about anyone who came to mind. For instance, that person whose name I could never remember. "That person, you know, the one whose name I flailed to catch, now what was she called?" I tried saying. Even in the dark I could feel Kinoko-san bristle with excitement at the word "flailed."

The next morning, Kinoko-san, her face striped in the

light coming in through the blinds, opened the large smile in the middle of her face, and murmured, "Well, I do believe I've finally afflailed."

It seemed as if I had finally afflailed, too. In the old days when I went into town, all sorts of delightful things to buy would leap into my field of vision. I rarely came home empty-handed. Now if I went, I found nothing I wanted to buy, nothing I wanted to eat. I didn't even really know what they were selling. I could see they were making all sorts of shapes out of translucent plastic. Sometimes I found them pretty, but I couldn't get a sense of what they were for. I thought I might understand if I deciphered the tiny letters covering the instruction booklets like ants, but I couldn't get myself in the mood to read. I didn't feel like eating either. Everything I ate was soft and smelled of monosodium glutamate, and I couldn't say whether it tasted good or bad. To tell the truth, I wasn't even in the mood to leave the house, but I didn't want to admit it, so I would go out, swinging my arms. I would say, "I'm going out for a bit. I mustn't just sit at home afflailing away the day." And Kinoko-san would narrow her eyes in a smile and say, "Have a nice time now." She didn't look envious. Probably it wasn't so much that she couldn't go out, but that she'd graduated from doing so. Out near the row of stores in front of the train station, hundreds of tin monkeys were smashing cymbals together. But it appeared that sounds were unable to penetrate within ten centimeters of my ears, so I didn't hear a thing. I said to my ear, nose and throat doctor, "Cities are so annoising, it's just as well my ears are getting hard of hearing."

Once I'd let myself say so, I suddenly couldn't remember whether there really was such an expression. Surely one's ears could not be hard. Ears are soft. If they are hard, they must have been cut off and given away, then must have hardened in their severed state. It was really too generous of me, giving away ears. Of course I only meant to lend them out, but apparently my intentions were misunderstood. My gestures are always too lavish and so this sort of thing is always happening. Or perhaps at the moment I really meant to sacrifice them, I can't remember.

I remember Kinoko-san saying once, "In my day, I too sacrificed my ears for another person, as one does in this world. But that person went far away." Far away might mean hell. One feels sorry for such people, but what can one do? A person who flees with another's ear ought simply to go to ear hell and turn into earwax. That's fate, and there's nothing one can do about it. One may wish to save such people, but what can one do about earwax?

The ear, nose and throat doctor, whatever he was thinking, suddenly said, "There isn't much we can do about minor hearing loss. If it gets too bad, you can wear whatever's needed."

I wondered where it was that the entrance to hell lay gaping open like an ear. I tried going out inside my head. On one side of the train station, a narrow road ran parallel to the tracks. There were stalls for ramen noodles and for pots of soup. There was an old bookstore and a record library. As I continued to walk, I began to feel as if hell had opened up in the shape of my ear. From a short distance away, it looked like a rain puddle that was starting to dry up, but when I got close, the dips and hollows of the green mud took on the shape of an earlobe.

I began to feel as if I wouldn't mind lending out just an earlobe. The inner ear I really didn't want to lend, but the outer part would be fine. I tried saying out loud, "A lobe? Certainly. My pleasure." At the time there was no one else in the room with me, but the flower wilting in its vase beside the window lifted its head to look at me, the curtain rose and fell and played against my cheek, and the ceiling began to perspire. I wondered whether I really was alone. Kinoko-san had said she was going to the hospital for an operation, which was apparently happening this very moment. If they didn't manage the operation properly and cut off some necessary part of her, she would not be coming back. If it came to that, I would donate a body part of my own. I could give at least one. Many of the body's organs come in twos. I have two ears. Two lungs. I think there might even be two of the uterus, I don't remember now. "There is the intestine, too. It's twelve fingers long. Surely you can spare one," I could hear the staff saying. "There is your twelve-layered court dress. Surely you can spare one, and you'll still be warm." I was cold. The windows were shut tight and the heater hummed, but the cold came creeping up from the floor into my bed.

Late that night Kinoko-san came home. She was lying upon a pedestal made of silver and covered with a pure white tablecloth. I pretended to be asleep and watched the whole thing. Kinoko-san seemed to have lost consciousness. The tablecloth was stained with strawberry jam.

The next day, for some reason, I didn't wake up till it was light outside. I felt the sunlight so strongly on my eyelids that I opened them, and saw Kinoko-san staring at me from one side. Startled, I tried to explain, "I'm so sorry, but I really can't lend you my ear. I don't have it any more, because they tricked me, and I never got it back." Kinoko-san smiled weakly and said, "Oh, my dear. How lamendacious, to lose your ear."

Apparently she was looking at where my ear used to be. I wondered how it looked. I couldn't see it because it was just out of my line of sight, but my ear really seemed to have been cut off. And it was Kinoko-san, not me, who was supposed to have had the operation. All last night I had surrendered to writhing creatures. Over and over again they had said to me, "We're coming with a knife, we're coming to get you, we're coming for an ear." I said, "I'll take a permanent marker and write protective poems on my ears." "Then we'll take your liver," they said. I was being oppressed by formless creatures. They clung to me on all sides and I couldn't shake them off. But I had never seen or felt my own liver, so I thought that maybe I would be fine without it. How pathetic, I thought, a person who'd never seen her own inner organs.

"My dear, have you never seen yourself?" Kinoko-san asked, laughing lightly. Dumbfounded, I replied evasively, "These days I don't even look in the mirror any more." "Well now, all you need is a hand mirror," Kinoko-san said, this time laughing like wind chimes. I held up my hand behind my neck, as if my nape would be reflected in my palm. Kinoko-san said, "You only look at your upper parts, don't you." Taken aback, I rummaged in the drawers for a hand mirror. I couldn't find one, so, relieved, I started looking for something I could use to change the subject. I used to have such an assortment of objects it was exhausting to organize them. What's funny is if now somebody asks me, "What objects, for instance?" I wouldn't be able to answer. I think they were in general useful things. Now I didn't have anything. What I finally found was a moldy wallet. It appeared to have some change inside, but I was too lazy to open it.

"My dear, have you really never looked at yourself?" Kinoko-san insisted. I couldn't very well ignore her, so I looked at her face and saw that her cheeks were flushed pink and her lips were burning. My answer was, "I understand. Please help me." But that night, and the next, no help arrived. I grew irritated at myself for just waiting. A woman who waits is too passive. After all, this wasn't a 1930s ballad. Thinking I would do something decisive at least inside my mouth, I picked up my toothbrush. With a Vivaldi violin concerto racing through my head, I attempted to move the toothbrush at a tremendous pace. My fingers stumbled over themselves, and it didn't go well. Giving up, I banged on the wall with my hand, which made quite a noise. But still I couldn't get out. I was trapped. Blood was throbbing in my temples. "What's the matter?" A worried face; I couldn't remember whose. "Such a noise, whatever is the matter?" She was speaking politely. As long as they are polite, I don't get very angry no matter what they say. "Such a noise? Surely you disheard," I replied, only my tongue stumbled over the words and I said "disheardened." "Now please stop, it's time for your meal."

"I'm simply afflailed." "So busy." "Just didn't manage." "Still, these days it does seem as if." When talking to a large company over dinner, one is not so much looking for things to say as walking along a narrow road trying not to touch things one shouldn't and somehow making one's way forward. If one says something wrong, the listener's mucous membranes are injured. The listener groans and opens his eyes wide. When one gets tired of seeing that, one clams up. When spoken to, one doesn't answer. One wishes, then, to be alone with Kinoko-san. One needn't watch one's words with Kinoko-san. On the other hand, one never knows what she will say next. "It twitches, you know. So interesting," she says, laughing. "But isn't it a little frightening?" I ask. "Oh no, not at all. After all, it's one's own, isn't it." "But what if somebody sees you?" "I don't fret about such things any more." "Isn't it a little frightening, it being for instance wet and all?" "Come now. It's not the least bit frightening. On a rainy day even the window is wet, after all."

Kinoko-san smelled different all at once. It turned out someone had made her a present of a Chanel perfume called Egoïste. "What a lovely scent, you've become a mis-recognizable beauty," I said. Kinoko-san laughed and gave me a look. When a person smells different, it's as if she's altogether a stranger, and one becomes a little shy. "It was a gift, you see, from a person I did something for." It seemed tactless to ask what the something was. She must have understood how I felt, since she added, "Diapers to bath, everything." I understood then that she was speaking of her son.

This so-called son, I must add, appeared only in conversation, and never in person. At dusk sometimes, when Kinoko-san's eyes lost their focus and stared into space, I would think, "She's thinking about him," and I would stare into space, too. I would see countless amoebas drifting in the air. They might have been nothing but the dust that plays in the liquid surrounding the eyeball. "Was there a visit?" I asked, but Kinoko-san didn't answer. So I reached over to the dry slice of bread on Kinoko-san's plate, and quickly pushed it into my mouth. On Sundays we had bread. At first I thought it was there to represent Christ's body, but it turned out that on Sundays the cook had the day off and wasn't there to cook the rice, so there was bread instead.

At dawn on Monday, when scattered footsteps began to disturb the ear's horizon, Kinoko-san suddenly said something like, "Isn't it strange to say 'packaged bread.' Isn't bread itself a kind of package?" I ignored her. At such times if I start to answer her, the other people might think I am at her level, and that would be frightening. The staff turned Kinoko-san's body over like a sheet of paper and said accusingly, "You didn't try the bread. There is no excretion, which suggests the bread wasn't eaten. You must have thrown it away somewhere." Kinoko-san only blinked her eyes with a puzzled air and said nothing. Three of them came over and tapped her back. A cloud of dust rose and Kinoko-san's back turned white. Kinoko-san narrowed her eyes with a look of great contentment, but I couldn't breathe with all the dust and began to cough. There was a great commotion, "Where's the bread? The bread? The bread?" One of them was bending over with a twisted neck to look under the bed. Another checked the window locks. O bread, o bread, why hast thou forsaken me?

The morning confusion subsided, and the staff disappeared. Somewhere a telephone is ringing. There is no receiver so I can't take the call. The people here are quite malicious, having a phone specially made with no receiver.

Still, it's better than nothing. Even if you can't take the call, a call is still a call. "It's ringing!" I think, and my upper body grows warm. Apparently there are still people who call me. After a while the telephone falls silent, without my having touched it. Then Kinoko-san's telephone begins to ring. I tap Kinoko-san's back, saying, "It's ringing, it's ringing." Kinoko-san pretends not to notice. She seems to want me to think she gets so many phone calls she needn't answer every one. I don't mind, but she's certain to regret it if she doesn't pick up out of pride, just when someone is trying to call. Perhaps in hell there is no telephone, and even if there is one, maybe no one will try to call. "They're calling, don't you hear?" I tap harder. Suddenly, someone pins my arms from behind. "Stop it. What are you thinking? You shouldn't hit people." Some juvenile delinquent girls are holding me back and shouting. These people don't like to see me keeping company with Kinoko-san, so every now and then they blow up. They are imprisoned by jealousy, envy and spite, so they quite often misunderstand one's actions. They don't have the ears to hear my explanations. To some extent, one has to forgive them on account of their youth, but I can't forgive people who use their youth as an excuse to oppress others. I see a palm in front of my eyes, so I bite it as hard as I can. My teeth impose themselves between thin bones set together like the sticks of a fan. There is a scream, and the hand flies up with amazing force, jerking my mouth along with it so that my jaw is almost dislocated, and after that I don't remember anything.

Again I wake up. I try to stifle my breathing, expecting Kinoko-san to start up again with her "Rend me your ear," but everything is completely silent, I don't hear a sound. I don't even hear Kinoko-san breathing. I want to turn on a light, but I can't bring myself to get up. Of course if I just lie here thinking about it, soon the sun will rise and the room will grow bright, but every day the sun comes up a little later than before. I get so tired of waiting I almost say, "Never mind. Dark is fine. Stay that way." If night were extended and it became quite normal to have one's morning and afternoon in the dark too, that would really be all right eventually. Since one's suffering is constituted by the waiting, having no light at all would be rather a relief. If it's always dark, I'll go out in the dark. If it's supposed to be dark, one isn't afraid of it anymore. The secretly glinting stars; the lights of distant cities. I rise in one smooth motion. My body is very light and I can get up without tensing any part of it. My head is strangely clear. The pain in my bones and the fever in my cheeks have subsided as if they had never been there, and like a dancer I stand on my toes on the bed. If I lift myself up a little, I might simply float away like mushroom spores. I give a little leap and my fingers touch the ceiling. It's tremendous fun. In front of my eyes stretches a row of trees that look like telephone poles. I hadn't noticed before that there were trees growing here. They are so tall I can't see their tops. High up on one of their trunks, Kinoko-san clings like a koala bear. Her left arm is twined around the eaves of the roof and she is waving with her right hand. Did she climb up so high all by herself, or did she leap from the window? "Do come up, dear, do join me," Kinoko-san sings, using the strange musical scale of a certain sort of bush warbler called something or other. Somehow, strength gathers in my shoulders and I find myself beginning to move my arms as if they were wings. I feel like flying, but my hips still seem too heavy for this. My head is heavy as a sandbag, too. If I fall, my hipbones will break and my skull will be shattered. When Kinoko-san's voice calls invitingly, "Do come," I feel that I cannot fall. Maybe if one simply gathers up one's courage to fly, one doesn't fall. Maybe when you alight on a voice, gravity fails. I have just placed my foot on the windowsill when I hear a huge commotion behind me. Cold hands suddenly insert themselves beneath my arms and I am pulled roughly back into the room. Palms smelling of soap become vivid flesh-colored butterflies flying around before my eyes. I find myself lying on the bed.

"We won't be able to meet any more, will we," Kinoko-san is singing far off, in the strange voice of a crow at sunset, but when in a panic I clutch at the window and pull myself up to look out, the trees that look like telephone poles are already gone.

CANNED FOREIGN

In any city one finds a surprisingly large number of people who cannot read. Some of them are still too young, others simply refuse to learn the letters of the alphabet. There are also a good many tourists and workers from other countries who live with a different set of characters altogether. In their eyes, the image of the city seems enigmatic, veiled.

I already knew the alphabet when I arrived in Hamburg, but I could gaze at the individual letters for a long time without recognizing the meaning of the words. For example, every day I looked at the same posters beside the bus stop but never read the names of the products. I know only that on one of the most beautiful of these posters the letter S appeared seven times. I don't think this letter reminded me of the shape of a snake. Not only the S, but all the other letters as well differed from live snakes in that they lacked both moisture and flesh. I repeated the S sounds in my mouth and noticed that my tongue suddenly tasted odd. I hadn't known a tongue, too, could taste of something.

The woman I met at this bus stop had a name that began with S: Sasha. I knew at once she couldn't read. Whenever she saw me she gazed at me intently and with interest, but she never attempted to read anything in my face. In those days I often found that people became uneasy when they couldn't read my face like a text.

It's curious the way the expression of a foreigner's face is often compared to a mask. Does this comparison conceal a wish to discover a familiar face behind the strange one?

Sasha complacently accepted all forms of illegibility. She didn't want to "read" things, she wanted to observe them, in detail. She must have been in her mid-fifties. I don't remember what color her hair was. I didn't learn to register hair-colors as a child, and so I still can't do this. Sasha often waited at the bus stop to meet her girlfriend. For Sonia—that's what she called her friend—was unable to get out of the bus on her own. Her arms and legs were incapable of working in unison toward a single goal, they couldn't all follow the same directions at once.

Sasha pressed Sonia's arms and legs together and called her name a few times, as though the name could bring harmony to her limbs.

Sasha and Sonia shared an apartment. Three times a

week someone came to attend to whatever written business there was. Apart from reading and writing, the two of them were able to manage everything they needed to live their lives.

A few times they had me over for coffee. There were questions Sasha and Sonia never asked, though I encountered these questions everywhere I went: mostly they began, "Is it true that the Japanese...." That is, most people wanted to know whether or not something they'd read in a newspaper or magazine was true. I was also often asked questions beginning, "In Japan do people also...." I was never able to answer them. Every attempt I made to describe the difference between two cultures failed: this difference was painted on my skin like a foreign script which I could feel but not read. Every foreign sound, every foreign glance, every foreign taste struck my body as disagreeable until my body changed. The Ö sounds, for example, stabbed too deeply into my ears and the R sounds scratched my throat. Certain expressions even gave me goose flesh, for instance "to get on his nerves," "fed up to here" or "all washed up."

Most of the words that came out of my mouth had nothing to do with how I felt. But at the same time I realized that my native tongue didn't have words for how I felt either. It's just that this never occurred to me until I'd begun to live in a foreign language.

Often it sickened me to hear people speak their native tongues fluently. It was as if they were unable to think and feel anything but what their language so readily served up to them.

From our bus stop one could see not only the various billboards but also the signs for a few restaurants. One of them belonged to a Chinese restaurant called "The Golden Dragon." Two Chinese characters shone gold and green. The first character meant "gold," and the second "dragon," I explained once to Sasha as I saw her staring at this sign. Sasha then pointed out that the second character was even shaped something like a "real" dragon. And in fact it *is* possible to see the image of a dragon in this character: the little box in the upper right-hand corner might be a dragon's head, and the lines on the right side remind me of a dragon's back. But Sasha knew it wasn't a "picture" of the dragon—she asked me whether I, too, could *write* it.

A few weeks later Sasha showed me a teacup and said that she'd discovered the "dragon" symbol on it. Indeed, the cup did bear this sign. Sasha had seen it in a shop and immediately bought it. For the first time in her life, she could read. Then I wanted to teach her some more characters. She'll always be illiterate, since she can't read the letters of the alphabet, but now she can read one character and knows that the alphabet isn't the only system of writing in the world.

Next to the bus stop was a small shop in which Sasha sometimes bought Sonia a bar of soap. Sonia loves soap, or, rather, she loves the packaging it comes in. The packaging was misleading: the paper on the outside was painted with butterflies, birds or flowers even though all it contained was soap. Very few products have pictures on the package that aren't immediately connected in some way to their contents. Sonia always unwrapped the soap right away when Sasha gave her some, then wrapped it up again.

Once the box the soap came in bore a phoenix on which the word "soap" was written in fine print that Sonia of course couldn't read. Sonia understood only the picture of the phoenix and the contents: soap.

Only because there is such a thing as written language, I thought to myself, could they paint a phoenix on the box instead of a piece of soap. What else could fix the meaning of its contents, the soap, if the letters weren't there? Then there would be the danger that the soap might, in the course of time, turn into a phoenix and fly away.

Once, in the supermarket, I bought a little can that had a Japanese woman painted on the side. Later, at home, I opened the can and saw inside it a piece of tuna fish. The woman seemed to have changed into a piece of fish during her long voyage. This surprise came on a Sunday: I had decided not to read any writing on Sundays. Instead I observed the people I saw on the street as though they were isolated letters. Sometimes two people sat down next to each other in a café, and thus, briefly, formed a word. Then they separated, in order to go off and form other words. There must have been a moment in which the combinations of these words formed, quite by chance, several sentences in which I might have read this foreign city like a text. But I never discovered a single sentence in this city, only letters and sometimes a few words that had no direct connection to any "cultural content." These words now and then led me to open the wrapping paper on the outside, only to find different wrapping paper below.

THE TALISMAN

In this city there are a great many women who wear bits of metal on their ears. They have holes put in their earlobes especially for this purpose. Almost as soon as I got here, I wanted to ask what these bits of metal on people's ears meant. But I didn't know if I could speak of this openly. My guidebook, for instance, says that in Europe you should never ask people you don't yet know very well anything related to their bodies or religion. Sometimes I thought these bits of metal—especially when I saw one in the form of a scythe, bow or anchor—might be a sort of talisman.

At first glance, the city doesn't strike me as particularly dangerous. Why, then, do so many women wear talismans on the street? Certainly it can get a bit spooky at times walking around the city alone. It's just that too few people live here. Even during the day I've often walked home from the train station without seeing anyone at all.

If these bits of metal are supposed to be a talisman, why are they so popular among women? I didn't know the name of the evil force these women were trying to protect themselves from with this talisman's help. They never revealed its name to me, and I still haven't made a concerted effort to find out what it is. Where I come from, people say you should never utter the name of a dangerous being aloud. If you do, this being will really appear. It has to be named indirectly. For example, you can simply replace its name with "it."

Gilda, a student who also lived in my building, always wore a triangular piece of metal on her ear. The first time we had a real conversation, she told me that a fifty-five-year-old librarian at the university had just committed suicide the day before. Up until her death, this librarian had fought to keep computers from being installed in her department. The woman couldn't have been intelligent, Gilda said, or she would have understood that computers are merely tools, not monsters. But apparently the computers weren't the cause of her suicide. She'd been suffering from severe depression for years. She'd lived alone, Gilda said, fingering her little triangle of metal.

"What is the meaning of that piece of metal?" I asked. She looked at me in surprise and asked whether I meant her "earring." The word "ring" had an unsettling effect on me. Gilda replied indifferently that the earring was simply a piece of jewelry and had no meaning at all.

As I had supposed, Gilda was reluctant to discuss the earring's significance. Instead she told me that highly educated women had holes put in their ears at a relatively late age, whereas working-class women started wearing earrings as girls.

I had read in a book that there are cultures in which part of the sexual organ is cut away during the initiation rite. A different part of the body can be substituted, however; the feet, for example, or the ears. In this case not the earring itself but merely the perforation of the earlobe would be significant.

But why was Gilda always so nervous? One day she placed two porcelain dogs on her windowsill. She refused to put the pots of flowers I'd given her there. These dogs were to sit on the windowsill all day long and stand guard over her apartment, like the stone dogs where I come from that guard the Shinto shrines. Gilda said she often had the feeling, when she was alone in the apartment, that a strange man was coming into her room through the window.

Once she knocked on my door in the middle of the night and said there was something wrong with her computer. I was really quite surprised she'd woken me up for this, since she knew I didn't know the first thing about computers. But soon I understood what the matter was:

Gilda claimed there was an alien being living inside her computer and producing sentences. She kept discovering sentences in her essays that she definitely hadn't written herself. But she refused to give me any examples; she said the sentences were indecent. I advised her to attach a talisman to her computer to make the evil force leave and keep new ones from coming. I used the term "evil force" because I didn't know what else to call it.

The talisman Gilda selected wasn't at all what I'd had in mind: I'd imagined something like a doll made of reeds or a piece of snakeskin. But Gilda went to a health food store and purchased three stickers. Each sticker bore an image that was no doubt intended to epitomize the evil force: a car, a nuclear power plant, a gun. And above each image stood the words: No thanks.

It struck me as overly polite to express gratitude while rejecting an evil force, but perhaps the word "thanks" was simply intended to avoid provoking the opponent's aggression.

Gilda pasted the stickers on the front of her computer, next to the screen, and appeared satisfied with them. A week later she bought three more stickers and put them on her bicycle, the refrigerator and the door of her apartment.

But I don't think she was completely reassured. Her computer, it's true, was now clean, but as if to make up for this, she began to feel as though an alien being were forcing its way into her body. She bought herself a sweater with a big tiger's head on it. Everyone who approached her had to brave the tiger's fierce gaze. Gilda also bought herself a jacket made from the skin of a dead animal. She wore tight pants printed in a leopard-skin pattern and a belt studded with several triangular bits of metal. It wouldn't have surprised me if she'd put on a mask with a lion's face.

Despite all this, her misgivings remained. At dinner, for instance, when she sat alone in the kitchen eating her soup, she suddenly had the impression that the soup contained everything she'd been trying to avoid all this time. She told me she'd decided to fast for a week or two. There were so many poisons in food, she explained, and, besides, she had too much excess flesh on her body. Gilda wasn't fat, but she was incapable of loving her own flesh because she sensed within it the presence of an alien element. She called this element "chemicals." Every culture has its own purification ceremony, or several of them. In this city, however, the ceremony has no predetermined day, time or opening prayer. There are no specifications, or at least no rules I could recognize as such. One day Gilda bought herself a book on fasting, and a few days later, when I met her on the stairs, she had already started. Her face looked less narrow than usual: it was almost round, as though there were water trapped beneath the skin. The piece of metal on her ear appeared heavier and colder than before. I swallowed the words I'd meant to say to her, for she seemed to me, all at once, like a stranger who—although I lived in her language—couldn't have understood me.

On her door flapped a sticker that was trying to come unstuck from the smooth metal.

RAISIN EYES

On Tuesdays I like to eat my father. He tastes of venison. Bread dough is what he's made of. I know he's really a woman. But you can't say this to his face or his eyes will turn hollow. When the fire is hot and the sun goes down, his dead brother whispers in his ear: you're a woman. He's made of bread dough. His nipples are raisins. The eyes of a woman he went to see in prison yesterday were also raisins. My father has black nipples. I've never seen them, they are buried deep in the flesh of his chest. Like mother and daughter they lie side by side in a cold sweat. Once a day they wake up and leap out of his flesh like a scream. My father tells me about them because he knows I'll like them. But he doesn't show them to me, he presses them back into place before I open my eyes. Usually I eat my bread cold. As I chew I feel the warmth of his flesh. I chew and chew and imagine I am continuing to chew. In reality I stop chewing and look around and find the raisins in the oven. They are burnt and smell like the shadow of a stag. A woman once lived in this house. When my father moved in, she was abducted. I can no longer recall the woman's face. I feel annoyed and go on eating. I sit down on the chair and go on eating. I like eating my father. It makes him think of the woman and repeat her words, which he taught to her: Whoever sits on the chair must want to stand. Whoever stands in the kitchen must want to fly. I could fly without effort if I stopped eating. But I go on eating and grow heavier and heavier. I wish I were made of raisins. In the language of raisins I say: do not call me by a place name. Do not give me women's shoes. It is the night of the festival of girls. My father gives me a woman's spoon. I can't sleep when my bed smells of burnt venison. My father tells me he used to be a man. When he ate bread from the oven, he became a woman. He shouldn't have told me that. I knew everything about him. The bread dough told me ages ago. Now we can no longer go on eating under one roof. I run away from home and have nothing left to eat. At the edge of town stands a house. The door is ajar. From the house comes the smell of venison. I go in and see a bed. It has three legs. In the bed lies my father, who can't possibly be here. His belly is soft and warm. In his belly, my mother sleeps. I'd have to wait a long time for her to be born. He doesn't want to let her go yet. Otherwise I'll have to keep eating away at his belly until I reach her. I stand in the garden and ask the apple tree what will become of her. I can hear two people breathing in unison. One sleeps in the other's belly. The belly is made of bread dough. I'm not hungry. I don't have to be hungry to want to eat the bread. It is dark now, and the lantern casts the shadow of a hunter. If it is my father, I will kill him before he can shoot the sleeping woman. It is my father. I have no gun. He gives a cry and falls. A fatal bullet is embedded in his belly as proof of the murder. I didn't do anything. From his belly, two raisin eyes peer out. Two people are dead, and the third survives.

STORYTELLERS WITHOUT SOULS

1

One of the German words I've become more and more attached to in recent years is the word *Zelle,* or "cell." This word lets me imagine a large number of tiny spaces alive within my body. Each space contains a voice that is telling a story. For this reason these cells can be compared to cells of other sorts: telephone booths, and the spaces inhabited by prisoners and monks.

It's beautiful when a phone booth is lit up at night on a dark street. In the section of Tokyo where I grew up, there was a park full of ginkgo trees. In one corner of the park stood a phone booth that was very popular with young girls. From dusk to midnight it was continuously occupied.

Probably the girls could develop their talent for telling stories better in this cell than at home with their parents. They gripped the receiver firmly and glanced around with lively, empty eyes, as if they could see the person they were talking to somewhere in the air. The transparent glass box, lit from within, where the girls spent so much time stood between the dark shapes of the trees in the park: this image fascinated me even then, when I myself was a girl. But the subject matter of the girls' conversations was of little interest. They spoke mostly about the males with whom they had relationships. Sometimes the phone booth resembled a transparent tree occupied by a tree spirit. The Japanese fairy tale "The Bamboo Princess" begins with an old man seeing a luminous bamboo trunk and chopping it down. Inside he discovers a newborn baby girl that he raises together with his wife. The tale ends with the girl, who has become a grown woman, flying back to where she really comes from: the moon.

The nocturnal phone booth might also have been a spaceship that has just landed in the park. The moon men have sent a moon girl to Earth to inform them about our life. The girl is just making her first report. What would she say about the park? Would she have much to report so soon after her arrival?

Later, in Austria, I saw a cell that immediately reminded me of the phone booth. It was made of solid wood and stood in the unlit corner of a Catholic church. The walls of the cell radiated warmth and calm; right away I thought I would be just as happy to stand inside telling stories as the girls in the phone booth. A friend told me the cell was called a "confessional" and that, like the nocturnal phone booth, it was a place to talk about sexual encounters. But unlike a modern phone booth, the confessional was made of wood and stood there like a tree whose roots have grown deep into the earth. It couldn't fly away like a spaceship. So there are storytelling cells that stay in one place, and others that appear to be mobile.

And so I understood why a chamber that resembles a prison cell is better suited for composing an erotic text than a large room in which optical sensuality is staged. I don't think much of asceticism, nor do I believe that sensual pleasure can enter a piece of writing only when it is suppressed in real life. The claim that a person who writes is not truly living can be made only by someone who sees a person and his life as subject and object. He might say the most important thing is to live one's life. I would say: I live, and my life lives as well. Even my writing lives. Thus the question of whether a person is living when he writes is misguided to begin with. One asks this sort of question only to make everything revolve around man.

It doesn't have anything to do with asceticism when someone sits in a cell and writes. It has much more to do with the activation of the living cells that comprise their own phone booths, monks' cells and prison cells within the body. Countless stories are told in these enclosed spaces. When I write, I try to hear the stories coming from within my body. When I listen, I realize how unfamiliar my own cells are to me. They consist of what I have inherited and what I have eaten. Thus it often happens that a story I hear within my body seems to me chronologically or geographically distant.

But can one understand the language of cells at all? The question brings to mind the image of yet another cell: the booth for simultaneous interpreters. At international congresses you often see these beautiful transparent booths in which people stand telling stories: they translate, so actually they are retelling tales that already exist. The lip movements and gestures of each interpreter and the way each of them glances about as she speaks are so various it's difficult to believe they are all translating a single, shared text. And perhaps it isn't really a single, shared text after all, perhaps the translators, by translating, demonstrate that this text is really many texts at once. The human body, too, contains many booths in which translations are made. I suspect that these are all translations for which no original exists. There are people, though, who assume that everyone is given an original text at birth. They call the place in which these texts are stored a soul.

Z

In Hamburg-on-the-Elbe there is a small harbor known as Devil's Bridge. A long time ago, no one was able to build a bridge across the Elbe strong enough to withstand a severe autumn storm. The devil made the desperate Hamburg merchants an offer: he would build an indestructible bridge. In payment he demanded a soul. The merchants promised to give him a soul when the bridge was completed. When the devil had finished work, it became apparent that none of the merchants was prepared to forfeit his soul, and so they sent a rat across the bridge to the devil, who stamped on the rat in fury and then sank into the earth. Since then the harbor has been called Devil's Bridge.

When I first heard this legend, I didn't understand it, because I didn't know rats have no souls. That is, rats have no souls for the devil, who is quite Christian in his orientation. In other religions that tell of the lives of plant souls and animal souls, a rat most certainly does have a soul—one every bit as precious as that of a Hamburg merchant. The devil needn't have been disappointed.

I have two ways of visualizing the human soul. In the first, the soul looks like an elongated roll I once ate in Tübingen. This sort of bread is called *Seele* or "soul" in Swabia, and many people have souls in this shape. But this doesn't mean the soul is inserted into their bodies like a roll.

The soul is an empty space in the body that must constantly be filled with the roll that has the same shape as this space, or with an embryo, or with the breath of love. Otherwise the owners of the souls feel as if something is missing.

The second way I picture the soul is as a fish whose name is also "sole": thus the soul is related to water, or to the sea. I'm thinking of something like the soul of a shaman. Among the Tungus, for example, it's said the soul of the aspiring shaman draws the tribal river down to the dwelling place of the shaman's ancestral spirits. There, among the roots of the tribe's shamanic tree, lies the shaman's animal mother, who devours the soul of the new arrival and then gives birth to it in the form of an animal. This animal can be a quadruped, or it can be a bird or a fish; in any case, it functions as the shaman's double and guardian spirit.

It's a nice thought that somewhere in the world the soul is leading its own life in animal form. The soul is independent from the person in question. The human being has no way of knowing what the soul is experiencing, but still there is a link between him and his soul. I would like to share a life with the person I call "my soul" as the shaman does with his: I never see or speak with this person, but everything I experience and write corresponds to this person's life. I appear to be soulless because my soul is constantly in transit.

3

In a book about Indians I once read that the soul cannot fly as fast as an airplane. Therefore one always loses one's soul on an airplane journey, and arrives at one's destination in a soulless state. Even the Trans-Siberian Railway travels more quickly than a soul can fly. The first time I came to Europe on the Trans-Siberian Railway, I lost my soul. When I boarded the train to go back, my soul was still on its way to Europe. I was unable to catch it. When I traveled to Europe once more, my soul was still making its way back to Japan. Later I flew back and forth so many times I no longer know where my soul is. In any case, this is a reason why travelers most often lack souls. And so tales of long journeys are always written without souls.

4

According to Walter Benjamin, there are two kinds of storytellers: "When someone goes on a trip, he has something to tell about, goes the German saying, and people imagine the storyteller as someone who has come from afar. But they enjoy no less listening to the man who has stayed at home, making an honest living, and who knows the local tales and traditions. If one wants to picture these two groups through their archaic representatives, one is embodied in the resident tiller of the soil, and the other in the trading seaman."

There are some who travel much farther than sailors and remain in one place even longer than the oldest farmer: the dead. And so there are no storytellers more interesting than the dead. But it is a problem that their language cannot be understood, it is not even audible. How can one hear the stories of the dead? This is one of the most difficult tasks of literature and is solved in different ways in various cultures.

A theater, for example, is often a place where the dead can speak. A simple example is found in *Hamlet*: the dead father comes on stage and tells how he was killed by his brother. That is the decisive moment in this play, without which neither Hamlet nor the audience would have access to the past. They would have to go on believing the story of the murderer, who claimed Hamlet's father had been bitten by a poisonous snake. Through the dead man's story we learn a bit of the past that otherwise would have remained obscure. The theater is the place where knowledge not accessible to us becomes audible. In other places, we almost always hear only the tales of the living. They force their stories on us to justify themselves, and so that they will be able to go on living, like Hamlet's uncle. The tales told by the dead are fundamentally different, because their stories are not told to conceal their wounds.

5

There are other places besides theaters where one can hear the stories of the dead: for example in an anthropological museum. At the Museum of Anthropology in Hamburg there are a number of transparent coffins lined up one beside the other, each containing a dead figure. Each figure personifies a tribe. A coffin standing on end resembles a phone booth because the figures inside look as if they are about to tell a story. That is probably why these coffins have to be standing up rather than lying flat, as coffins usually do.

The figures in the coffins—dolls made of plastic—bear witness to the link between death and these dolls: all of the tribes represented in the form of dolls were, at some point in history, culturally or economically conquered by others and to some extent destroyed. As in other museums as well, a power relationship is illustrated here: that which is represented is always something that has been destroyed. In a zoological museum, for example, a stuffed wolf might be put on display, whereas no wolf can display a human being.

Historical museums, too, are marked by a hierarchical relationship between past and present.

As long as an outsider appears threatening, the others try to destroy him. When he is dead, he can be lovingly represented as a doll in a museum. One can look at the doll, listen to the explanations of its way of life, view the photos of its homeland, but there is always something that remains unclear. There is a veil separating the museum visitor from the dead doll, making it impossible to learn much. One learns much more when one attempts to describe an imaginary tribe. What should their lives look like? How does their language function? What is this completely unfamiliar social system like? It is equally interesting to play the role of an observer who comes from a fictional culture. How would he describe "our" world? This is the endeavor of fictive ethnology, in which not the described but the describer is imaginary.

6

That the dolls can be thought of only in conjunction with death can be seen in the following brief example: a long time ago, when the people in many Japanese villages were suffering inescapable poverty, it sometimes happened that women who gave birth to children, rather than starving together with them, would kill them at birth. For each child that was put to death, a wooden doll called *kokeshi,* meaning make-the-child-go-away, was crafted, so that the people would never forget they had survived at the expense of these children.

7

It is difficult to understand the language of dolls. To our ears, they are usually mute. The language of the dead isn't really comprehensible either. For the most part it can't even be heard. Only in a state in which one is not fixated on understanding can one hear it.

I remember a day when I felt as though I'd heard the language of the dead. In 1982, in the spring, I visited a village in Nepal inhabited by Tibetans. Before me stood a temple from which a prayer was emanating. When I listened more closely, I realized it consisted of several voices. I looked inside the temple and saw a single monk praying. From his body came several voices. After he had taken a breath, he once more spread out a deep voice like a carpet on which several other voices could then appear. He produced these voices from within his body, offering a sounding board to storytellers who themselves had none. The dead, for example, who had no bodies of their own in which their voices could resonate, were able to become audible in the voice of the monk.

At the time I tried to produce my own voice carpet. I failed in my attempt, but for the first time I became conscious of several secondary voices that form part of my speech. I began to pay attention to these voices as I spoke. Telling stories no longer took the place of listening; rather, listening gave rise to stories.

Perhaps the ear is the organ of storytelling, not the mouth. Why else was the poison poured into the ear of Hamlet's father rather than his mouth? To cut off a person from the world, you must first destroy not his mouth but his ear.

8

There are even dolls that can articulate the language of the living. In 1992 I visited London to see them. It wasn't only the popular singing and speaking wax figures of rock musicians that could speak our language, there were also several less famous mechanical dolls in the guise of a fortune teller or a doctor. I found a mechanical doctor at a marketplace. When I sat down opposite him, he told me in a mechanical voice to place my hands on the glass plate. Between us stood a desk topped with a glass plate through which one could observe his fascinating mechanism. The creases in my palm were read, that is, they were deciphered like letters of the alphabet. The doctor nodded and picked up a slip of paper with a precise gesture. He wrote out a prescription and gave it to me. Unfortunately, his handwriting was illegible. A furiously wavy line traversed the paper from left to right. This, then, is what the translation of the creases in my palm into a particular language looked like. I pretended I was able to read this writing, thanked the mechanical doctor and went on my way.

TONGUE DANCE

My tongue is always somewhat swollen when I wake up, much too large to move easily within my mouth. It blocks my windpipe, I can feel the pressure building up in my lungs. How much longer do I have to suffocate? I wonder, and at once it begins to shrink. At such moments, my tongue reminds me of a worn-out sponge: dry and stiff, it retreats into my esophagus, dragging the rest of my head behind it.

Once in a dream I was standing on a deserted highway. My entire body was one huge tongue. Far off in the distance, I could see a man in uniform lying on his stomach. I told myself I hadn't seen anything. Tongues don't have eyes. Then two policemen appeared from nowhere and spoke to me. They said I was the only one who could have witnessed this brutal murder. Shooting a uniform in the back carried a severe penalty. In reality, the man lying on the ground was a tin soldier. There was a lit cigarette sticking out of the pocket of his metal trousers.

I was a tongue. I left the house just as I was: naked, pink and unbearably moist. It was easy to delight people I met on the street, but no one was willing to touch me. The shop windows were full of plastic women who lacked sexual organs. The prices on the tags had been crossed out with red ink. Vigilant citizens are careful not to touch any tongues that haven't been wrapped up in plastic. My entire person now consisted of one huge tongue. I was unable to find work. Then I wrote an autobiography. The life story of a tongue. I read it aloud to audiences in Melsungen, Hemmelsdorf, Winsen, Bad Hersfeld, Bendestorf, Reutlingen and Ittingen.

For several weeks now I've had difficulties each time I give a reading: the letters on the pages of my manuscript transform themselves into a wall. I walk patiently along this wall, but there is no door, no window, not even a bell to ring. I can't read the sentences, even though I'm the one who wrote them. (But how can I use the word "I" so carelessly? As each line is completed, it pulls back from me and is transformed into a language I no longer understand.)

Unsure of what to do, I begin to force out the first few words. Each one is a hurdle. If only the text didn't have any words in it, I think, I'd be able to read it easily. The wall of letters blocks my view. Sometimes the sentences break off so suddenly I nearly tumble into the hole of the period. And no sooner have I gotten beyond this danger than the next sentence is already standing there in front of me, with no visible entryway. How am I to begin? The words are becoming more and more angular, unwieldy. Soon the individual letters are sprouting out of them in all directions. Where does a word begin? Where does it end? My courage, which consists of one huge tongue, shrinks until it is smaller than a comma. I have to clamber up each of the letters with my tiny feet, unable to see what lies behind it. Each sound plunges me into an abyss. My voice becomes softer and softer, while the written characters become louder and louder.

I am sick. My entire illness consists of one huge tongue. I look under "doctors" in the phone book but don't know which one to call. My old dentist hated tongues because they interfered with his examinations. My internist ought to be interested in tongues, since they reveal the condition of the stomach. But he never let me show him my tongue. I turn a few more pages in the phone book. Finally, under the heading "language," I find a language doctor.

The next day I call the language doctor and go to his office. I tell him about plunging into the abyss and my language pains. This man in his white smock immediately interrupts me and starts making recommendations. In each sentence I say, I am to select a single word I wish to emphasize. This word, he says, should dominate over the others and take complete control of the sentence, otherwise anarchy will reign in my oral cavity. I am to focus on this single word and skim over all the others with a light breath. Suddenly my tongue starts to speak in Japanese.

Not like that, he says, select a word to emphasize. But I can't pick out a single word at the expense of all the others. It's not that it offends my sense of democracy, but the rhythm of my breathing trips me up. The doctor is insistent. It really is necessary, he says, for me to emphasize a single word, not by raising the pitch of my voice, but by giving this word greater weight. Once again, Japanese words begin to spring out of my larynx, or are my vocal cords a tape running in some strange machine?

Not like that, the doctor says, hold the pitch steady, otherwise it sounds indecent. In the world of phonetics, pitches are like prostitutes. Besides, "b" isn't supposed to sound like a spring wind creeping up behind your back; it should make an explosive entrance. In the word "bed," for instance: one should leap into bed in a single bound, not creep in furtively.

Following the doctor's instructions, I begin to emphasize only these few chosen words, and all at once the letters of stone vanish. How strange! In order to read, I have to look at the text. But to avoid stumbling, I have to pretend the letters don't exist. This is the secret of the alphabet: the letters aren't there any longer, and at the same time they haven't yet vanished.

In a dream, I meet Zoltán in the street. I invite him to have tea with me. It's getting dark. In the light of a neon lamp, his face looks pale. What's the matter? I ask. His skin has become nearly transparent, and beneath it his red and blue veins appear like written characters. On the bare flesh of his inner thigh, I see an "n." What is that? I ask. Embarrassed, Zoltán replies that he's become so thin he can no longer cover his blood with flesh. In the chilly air of the dark room, his skin becomes more and more transparent, as if it were covered with ice. I'm glad I have on a fur coat. Is it a tattoo? I ask him warily. No, it's just my nature, he murmurs. But what about that "n"? That can't be just nature.

He says that when I say "n," I shouldn't press the back of my tongue against my palate; the tip of my tongue is supposed to press against the back of my front teeth. Otherwise you can't hear this consonant at all, and I would be cutting off the end of his name.

No, not like that, he says, the "n" is supposed to sound different. But for me, this is physically impossible. If the "n" isn't followed by a vowel, I can't coax my tongue back to the front of my mouth. Therefore I can't, for example, pronounce the word "want," because my tongue is pressing not against the consonants but against Zoltán's soft penis.

It appears to be true that nothing can cover his transparent skin any longer. I watch as countless tiny letters flow into the organ. If only there were an "o" in between! It would be easy for me to say "wanot." So why shouldn't I say "wanot" instead of "want"? If some day I no longer need the "o," I can just drop it. Until then, I'll keep my wanot. The penis is becoming harder and harder, its surface feels smooth, like silk cloth. Perhaps a person, to be a friend, has to want, to wish for something in the future; but I'm not a friend, I'm a tongue. In any case, I can't pronounce the word "friend" because there's a single "n" in the middle of it. "Frienod!" I cry out. At this moment, Zoltán's penis explodes. Liquid characters spurt out of it, gleam briefly in the neon light and vanish again amid the silence of mute taste buds.

WHERE EUROPE BEGINS

1

For my grandmother, to travel was to drink foreign water. Different places, different water. There was no need to be afraid of foreign landscapes, but foreign water could be dangerous. In her village lived a girl whose mother was suffering from an incurable illness. Day by day her strength waned, and her brothers were secretly planning her funeral. One day as the girl sat alone in the garden beneath the tree, a white serpent appeared and said to her: "Take your mother to see the Fire Bird. When she has touched its flaming feathers, she will be well again." "Where does the Fire Bird live?" asked the girl. "Just keep going west. Behind three tall mountains lies a bright shining city, and at its center, atop a high tower, sits the Fire Bird." "How can we ever reach this city if it is so far off? They say the mountains are inhabited by monsters." The serpent replied: "You needn't be afraid of them. When you see them, just remember that you, too, like all other human beings, were once a monster in one of your previous lives. Neither hate them nor do battle with them, just continue on your way. There is only one thing you must remember: when you are in the city where the Fire Bird lives, you must not drink a single drop of water." The girl thanked him, went to her mother and told her everything she had learned. The next day the two of them set off. On every mountain they met a monster that spewed green, yellow and blue fire and tried to burn them up; but as soon as the girl reminded herself that she, too, had once been just like them, the monsters sank into the ground. For ninety-nine days they wandered through the forest, and finally they reached the city, which shone brightly with a strange light. In the burning heat, they saw a tower in the middle of this city, and atop it sat the Fire Bird. In her joy, the girl forgot the serpent's warning and drank water from the pond. Instantly the girl became ninety-nine years old and her mother vanished in the flaming air.

When I was a little girl, I never believed there was such a thing as foreign water, for I had always thought of the globe as a sphere of water with all sorts of small and large islands swimming on it. Water had to be the same everywhere. Sometimes in sleep I heard the murmur of the water that flowed beneath the main island of Japan. The border surrounding the island was also made of water that ceaselessly beat against the shore in waves. How can one say where the place of foreign water begins when the border itself is water?

Z

The crews of three Russian ships stood in uniform on the upper deck playing a farewell march whose unfamiliar solemnity all at once stirred up the oddest feelings in me. I, too, stood on the upper deck, like a theatergoer who has mistakenly stepped onstage, for my eyes were still watching me from among the crowd on the dock, while I myself stood blind and helpless on the ship. Other passengers threw long paper snakes in various colors toward the dock. The red streamers turned midair into umbilical cords—one last link between the passengers and their loved ones. The green streamers became serpents and proclaimed their warning, which would probably only be forgotten on the way, anyhow. I tossed one of the white streamers into the air. It became my memory. The crowd slowly withdrew, the music faded, and the sky grew larger behind the mainland. The moment my paper snake disintegrated, my memory ceased to function. This is why I no longer remember anything of this journey. The fifty hours aboard the ship to the harbor town in Eastern Siberia, followed by the hundred and sixty hours it took to reach Europe on the Trans-Siberian Railroad, have become a blank space in my life which can be replaced only by a written account of my journey.

3

Diary excerpt:

The ship followed the coastline northward. Soon it was dark, but many passengers still sat on the upper deck. In the distance one could see the lights of smaller ships. "The fishermen are fishing for squid," a voice said behind me. "I don't like squid. When I was little, we had squid for supper every third night. What about you?" another voice asked. "Yes," a third one responded, "I ate them all the time, too. I always imagined they were descended from monsters." "Where did you grow up?" the first voice asked.

Voices murmured all around me, tendrils gradually entwining. On board such a ship, everyone begins putting together a brief autobiography, as though he might otherwise forget who he is.

"Where are you going?" the person sitting next to me

asked. "I'm on my way to Moscow." He stared at me in surprise. "My parents spoke of this city so often I wanted to see it with my own eyes." Had my parents really talked about Moscow? On board such a ship, everyone begins to lie. The man was looking so horrified I had to say something else right away. "Actually I'm not so interested in Moscow itself, but I want to have experienced Siberia." "What do you want to experience in Siberia?" he asked, "What is there in Siberia?" "I don't know yet. Maybe nothing to speak of. But the important thing for me is traveling *through* Siberia." The longer I spoke, the more unsure of myself I became. He went to sit beside another passenger, leaving me alone with the transparent word *through*.

4

A few months before I set off on my journey, I was working evenings after school in a food processing factory. A poster adverstising a trip to Europe on the Trans-Siberian Railroad transformed the immeasurably long distance to Europe into a finite sum of money.

In the factory, the air was kept at a very low temperature so the meat wouldn't go bad. I stood in this cold, which I referred to as "Siberian frost," wrapping frozen poultry in plastic. Beside the table stood a bucket of hot water in which I could warm my hands at intervals.

Once three frozen chickens appeared in my dreams. I watched my mother place them in the frying pan. When the pan was hot, they suddenly came to life and flew out the kitchen window. "No wonder we never have enough to eat," I said with such viciousness even I was shocked. "What am I supposed to do?" my mother asked, weeping.

Besides earning money, there were two other things I wanted to do before my departure: learn Russian and write an account of the journey. I always wrote a travel narrative before I set off on a trip, so that during the journey I'd have something to quote from. I was often speechless when I traveled. This time it was particularly useful that I'd written my report beforehand. Otherwise, I wouldn't have known what to say about Siberia. Of course, I might have quoted from my diary, but I have to admit that I made up the diary afterward, having neglected to keep one during the journey.

5

Excerpt from my first travel narrative:

Our ship left the Pacific and entered the Sea of Japan, which separates Japan from Eurasia. Since the remains of Siberian mammoths were discovered in Japan, there have been claims that a land bridge once linked Japan and

Siberia. Presumably, human beings also crossed from Siberia to Japan. In other words, Japan was once part of Siberia.

In the *Atlas of the World* in the ship's library I looked up Japan, this child of Siberia that had turned its back on its mother and was now swimming alone in the Pacific. Its body resembled that of a seahorse, which in Japanese is called *Tatsu-no-otoshigo*—the lost child of the dragon.

Next to the library was the dining room, which was always empty during the day. The ship rolled on the stormy seas, and the passengers stayed in bed. I stood alone in the dining room, watching plates on the table slide back and forth without being touched. All at once I realized I had been expecting this stormy day for years, since I was a child.

6

Something I told a woman three years after the journey:

At school we often had to write essays, and sometimes these included "dream descriptions." Once I wrote about the dream in which my father had red skin.

My father comes from a family of merchants in Osaka. After World War II, he came to Tokyo with all he owned: a bundle containing, among other things, an alarm clock. This clock, which he called the "Rooster of the

Revolution," soon stopped running, but as a result, it showed the correct time twice each day, an hour that had to be returned to twice a day anyhow. "Time runs on its own, you don't need an alarm clock for that," he always said in defense of his broken clock, "and when the time comes, the city will be so filled with voices of the oppressed that no one will be able to hear a clock ring any longer."

His reasons for leaving the land of his birth he always explained to his relatives in a hostile tone: "Because he was infected with the Red Plague." These words always made me think of red, inflamed skin.

A huge square, crowds of people strolling about. Some of them had white hair, others green or gold, but all of them had red skin. When I looked closer, I saw that their skin was not inflamed but rather inscribed with red script. I was unable to read the text. No, it wasn't a text at all but consisted of many calendars written on top of each other. I saw numberless stars in the sky. At the tip of the tower, the Fire Bird sat observing the motion in the square.

This must have been "Moscow," I wrote in my essay, which my teacher praised without realizing I had invented the dream. But then what dream is not invented?

•

Later I learned that for a number of leftists in Western Europe this city had a different name: Peking.

7

Diary excerpt:

The ship arrived in the harbor of the small Eastern Siberian town Nachodka. The earth seemed to sway beneath my feet. No sooner had I felt the sensation of having put a border, the sea, behind me than I glimpsed the beginning of the train tracks that stretched for ten thousand kilometers.

That night I boarded the train. I sat down in a four-bed compartment where I was soon joined by two Russians. The woman, Masha, offered me pickled mushrooms and told me she was on her way to visit her mother in Moscow. "Ever since I got married and moved to Nachodka, my mother has been *behind* Siberia," she said. Siberia, then, is the border between here and there, I thought, such a wide border!

I lay down on the bed on my belly and gazed out the window. Above the outlines of thousands of birches I saw numberless stars that seemed about to tumble down. I took out my pocket notebook and wrote:

When I was a baby, I slept in a Mexican hammock. My parents had bought the hammock not because they found it romantic, but because the apartment was so cramped that there was no room for me except in the air. All there was in the apartment was seven thousand books whose stacks lined the three walls all the way to the ceiling. At night they turned into trees thick with foliage. When a large truck drove past the house, my Mexican hammock swung in the forest. But during the minor earthquakes that frequently shook the house, it remained perfectly still, as though there were an invisible thread connecting it to the subterranean water.

8

Diary excerpt:

When the first sun rose over Siberia, I saw an infinitely long row of birches. After breakfast I tried to describe the landscape, but couldn't. The window with its tiny curtains was like the screen in a movie theater. I sat in the front row, and the picture on the screen was too close and too large. The segment of landscape was repeated, constantly changing, and refused me entry. I picked up a collection of Siberian fairy tales and began to read.

In the afternoon I had tea and gazed out the window

again. Birches, nothing but birches. Over my second cup of tea I chatted with Masha, not about the Siberian landscape but about Moscow and Tokyo. Then Masha went to another compartment, and I remained alone at the window. I was bored and began to get sleepy. Soon I was enjoying my boredom. The birches vanished before my eyes, leaving only the again-and-again of their passage, as in an imageless dream.

9

Excerpt from my first travel narrative:

Siberia, "the sleeping land" (from the Tartar: *sib* = sleep, *ir* = Earth), but it wasn't asleep. So it really wasn't at all necessary for the prince to come kiss the Earth awake. (He came from a European fairy tale.) Or did he come to find treasure?

When the Creator of the Universe was distributing treasures on Earth and flew over Siberia, he trembled so violently with cold that his hands grew stiff and the precious stones and metals he held in them fell to the ground. To hide these treasures from Man, he covered Siberia with eternal frost.

It was August, and there was no trace of the cold that had stiffened the Creator's hands. The Siberian tribes mentioned in my book were also nowhere to be seen, for the Trans-Siberian Railroad traverses only those regions populated by Russians—tracing out a path of conquered territory, a narrow extension of Europe.

10

Something I told a woman three years after the journey:

For me, Moscow was always the city where you never arrive. When I was three years old, the Moscow Artists' Theater performed in Tokyo for the first time. My parents spent half a month's salary on tickets for Chekhov's *Three Sisters*.

When Irina, one of the three sisters, spoke the famous words: "To Moscow, to Moscow, to Moscow...," her voice pierced my parents' ears so deeply that these very same words began to leap out of their own mouths as well. The three sisters never got to Moscow, either. The city must have been hidden somewhere backstage. So it wasn't Siberia, but rather the theater stage that lay between my parents and the city of their dreams.

In any case, my parents, who were often unemployed during this period, occasionally quoted these words. When my father, for example, spoke of his unrealistic plan of founding his own publishing house, my mother would say, laughing, "To Moscow, to Moscow, to Moscow...." My father would say the same thing whenever my mother spoke of her childhood in such a way as though she might be able to become a child again. Naturally, I didn't understand what they meant. I only sensed that the word had something to do with impossibility. Since the word "Moscow" was always repeated three times, I didn't even know it was a city and not a magic word.

11

Diary excerpt:

I flipped through a brochure the conductor had given me. The photographs showed modern hospitals and schools in Siberia. The train stopped at the big station at Ulan-Ude. For the first time, there were many faces in the train that were not Russian.

I laid the brochure aside and picked up my book.

A fairy tale told among the Tungus:

Once upon a time there was a shaman who awakened all the dead and wouldn't let even a single person die. This made him stronger than God. So God suggested a contest: by magic words alone, the shaman was to transform two pieces of chicken meat given him by God into live chickens. If the shaman failed, he wouldn't be stronger than God any longer. The first piece of meat was transformed into a chicken by the magic words and flew away, but not the second one. Ever since, human beings have died. Mostly in hospitals.

Why was the shaman unable to change the second piece of meat into a chicken? Was the second piece somehow different from the first, or did the number two rob the shaman of his power? For some reason, the number two always makes me uneasy.

I also made the acquaintance of a shaman, but not in Siberia; it was much later, in a museum of anthropology in Europe. He stood in a glass case, and his voice came from a tape recorder that was already rather old. For this reason his voice always quavered prodigiously and was louder than a voice from a human body. The microphone is an imitation of the flame that enhances the voice's magical powers.

Usually, the shamans were able to move freely between the three zones of the world. That is, they could visit both the heavens and the world of the dead just by climbing up and down the World-Tree. My shaman, though, stood not in one of these three zones, but in a fourth one: the museum. The number four deprived him permanently of his power: his face was frozen in an expression of fear, his mouth, half-open, was dry, and in his painted eyes burned no fire.

12

Excerpt from my first travel narrative:

In the restaurant car I ate a fish called *omul'*. Lake Baikal is also home to several other species that actually belong in a saltwater habitat, said a Russian teacher sitting across from me—the Baikal used to be a sea.

But how could there possibly be a sea here, in the middle of the continent? Or is the Baikal a hole in the continent that goes all the way through? That would mean my childish notion about the globe being a sphere of water was right after all. The water of the Baikal, then, would be the surface of the water-sphere. A fish could reach the far side of the sphere by swimming through the water.

And so the *omul'* I had eaten swam around inside my body that night, as though it wanted to find a place where its journey could finally come to an end.

13

There were once two brothers whose mother, a Russian painter, had emigrated to Tokyo during the Revolution and lived there ever since. On her eightieth birthday she expressed the wish to see her native city, Moscow, once more before she died. Her sons arranged for her visa and accompanied her on her journey on the Trans-Siberian Railroad. But when the third sun rose over Siberia, their mother was no longer on the train. The brothers searched for her from first car to last, but they couldn't find her. The conductor told them the story of an old man who, three years earlier, had opened the door of the car, mistaking it for the door to the toilet, and had fallen from the train. The brothers were granted a special visa and traveled the same stretch in the opposite direction on the local train. At each station they got out and asked whether anyone had seen their mother. A month passed without their finding the slightest trace.

I can remember the story up to this point; afterwards I must have fallen asleep. My mother often read me stories that filled the space between waking and sleep so completely that, in comparison, the time when I was awake lost much of its color and force. Many years later I found, quite by chance, the continuation of this story in a library.

The old painter lost her memory when she fell from the train. She could remember neither her origins nor her plans. So she remained living in a small village in Siberia that seemed strangely familiar to her. Only at night, when she heard the train coming, did she feel uneasy, and sometimes she even ran alone through the dark woods to the tracks, as though someone had called to her.

14

As a child, my mother was often ill, just like her own mother, who had spent half her life in bed. My mother grew up in a Buddhist temple in which one could hear, as early as five o'clock in the morning, the prayer that her father, the head priest of the temple, was chanting with his disciples.

One day, as she sat alone under a tree reading a novel, a student who had come to visit the temple approached her and asked whether she always read such thick books. My mother immediately replied that what she'd like best was a novel so long she could never finish it, for she had no other occupation but reading.

The student considered a moment, then told her that in the library in Moscow there was a novel so long that no one could read all of it in a lifetime. This novel was not only long, but also as cryptic and cunning as the forests of Siberia, so that people got lost in it and never found their way out again once they'd entered. Since then, Moscow has been the city of her dreams, its center not Red Square, but the library.

This is the sort of thing my mother told me about her childhood. I was still a little girl and believed in neither the infinitely long novel in Moscow nor the student who might have been my father. For my mother was a good liar and told lies often and with pleasure. But when I saw her sitting and reading in the middle of the forest of books, I was afraid she might disappear into a novel. She never rushed through books. The more exciting the story became, the more slowly she read.

She never actually wanted to arrive at any destination at all, not even "Moscow." She would greatly have preferred for "Siberia" to be infinitely large. With my father things were somewhat different. Although he never got to Moscow, either, he did inherit money and founded his own publishing house, which bore the name of this dream city.

15

Diary excerpt:

There were always a few men standing in the corridor smoking strong-smelling Stolica cigarettes (*stolica* = capital city).

"How much longer is it to Moscow?" I asked an old man who was looking out the window with his grandchild.

"Three more days," he responded and smiled with eyes that lay buried in deep folds.

So in three days I would really have crossed Siberia and would arrive at the point where Europe begins? Suddenly I noticed how afraid I was of arriving in Moscow.

"Are you from Vietnam?" he asked.

"No, I'm from Tokyo."

His grandchild gazed at me and asked him in a low voice: "Where is Tokyo?" The old man stroked the child's head and said softly but clearly: "In the East." The child was silent and for a moment stared into the air as though a city were visible there. A city it would probably never visit.

Hadn't I also asked questions like that when I was a child? —Where is Peking? —In the West. —And what is in the East, on the other side of the sea? —America.

The world sphere I had envisioned was definitely not round, but rather like a night sky, with all the foreign places sparkling like fireworks.

16

During the night I woke up. Rain knocked softly on the windowpane. The train went slower and slower. I looked out the window and tried to recognize something in the darkness.... The train stopped, but I couldn't see a station. The outlines of the birches became clearer and clearer, their skins brighter, and suddenly there was a shadow moving between them. A bear? I remembered that many Siberian tribes bury the bones of bears so they can be resurrected. Was this a bear that had just returned to life?

The shadow approached the train. It was not a bear but a person. The thin figure, face half concealed beneath wet hair, came closer and closer with outstretched arms. I saw the beams of three flashlights off to the left. For a brief moment, the face of the figure was illumined: it was an old woman. Her eyes were shut, her mouth open, as though she wanted to cry out. When she felt the light on her, she gave a shudder, then vanished in the dark woods.

This was part of the novel I wrote before the journey and read aloud to my mother. In this novel, I hadn't built a secret pathway leading home for her; in contrast to the novel in Moscow, it wasn't very long.

"No wonder this novel is so short," my mother said. "Whenever a woman like that shows up in a novel, it always ends soon, with her death."

"Why should she die. *She* is Siberia."

"Why is Siberia a *she*? You're just like your father, the two of you only have one thing in your heads: going to Moscow."

"Why don't *you* go to Moscow?"

"Because then you wouldn't get there. But if I stay here, you can reach your destination."

"Then I won't go, I'll stay here."

"It's too late. You're already on your way."

17

Excerpt from the letter to my parents:

Europe begins not in Moscow but somewhere before. I looked out the window and saw a sign as tall as a man with two arrows painted on it, beneath which the words "Europe" and "Asia" were written. The sign stood in the middle of a field like a solitary customs agent.

"We're in Europe already!" I shouted to Masha, who was drinking tea in our compartment.

"Yes, everything's Europe behind the Ural Mountains," she replied, unmoved, as though this had no importance, and went on drinking her tea.

I went over to a Frenchman, the only foreigner in the car besides me, and told him that Europe didn't just begin in Moscow. He gave a short laugh and said that Moscow was not Europe.

18

Excerpt from my first travel narrative:

The waiter placed my borscht on the table and smiled at Sasha, who was playing with the wooden doll Matroshka next to me. He removed the figure of the round farmwife from its belly. The smaller doll, too, was immediately taken apart, and from its belly came—an expected surprise—an even smaller one. Sasha's father, who had been watching his son all this time with a smile, now looked at me and said: "When you are in Moscow, buy a Matroshka as a souvenir. This is a typically Russian toy."

Many Russians do not know that this "typically Russian" toy was first manufactured in Russia at the end of the nineteenth century, modeled after ancient Japanese dolls. But I don't know what sort of Japanese doll could have been the model for Matroshka. Perhaps a *kokeshi*, which my grandmother once told me the story of. A long time ago, when the people of her village were still suffering from extreme poverty, it sometimes happened that women who gave birth to children, rather than starving together with them, would kill them at birth. For each child that was put to death, a *kokeshi*, meaning make-the-child-go-away, was crafted, so that the people would never forget they had survived at the expense of these children. To what story might people connect Matroshka some day? Perhaps with the story of the souvenir, when people no longer know what souvenirs are.

"I'll buy a Matroshka in Moscow," I said to Sasha's father. Sasha extracted the fifth doll and attempted to take it, too, apart. "No, Sasha, that's the littlest one," his father cried. "Now you must pack them up again."

The game now continued in reverse. The smallest doll

vanished inside the next-smallest one, then this one inside the next, and so on.

In a book about shamans, I had once read that our souls can appear in dreams in the form of animals or shadows or even dolls. The Matroshka is probably the soul of the travelers in Russia who, sound asleep in Siberia, dream of the capital.

19

I read a Samoyedic fairy tale:

Once upon a time there was a small village in which seven clans lived in seven tents. During the long, hard winter, when the men were off hunting, the women sat with their children in the tents. Among them was a woman who especially loved her child.

One day she was sitting with her child close beside the fire, warming herself. Suddenly a spark leapt out of the fire and landed on her child's skin. The child began to cry. The woman scolded the fire: "I give you wood to eat and you make my child cry! How dare you? I'm going to pour water on you!" She poured water on the fire, and so the fire went out.

It grew cold and dark in the tent, and the child began to cry again. The woman went to the next tent to fetch new fire, but the moment she stepped into the tent, this fire, too, went out. She went on to the next one, but here the same thing happened. All seven fires went out, and the village was dark and cold.

"Do you realize we're almost in Moscow?" Masha asked me. I nodded and went on reading.

When the grandmother of this child heard what had happened, she came to the tent of the woman, squatted down before the fire and gazed deep into it. Inside, on the hearth, sat an ancient old woman, the Empress of Fire, with blood on her forehead. "What has happened? What should we do?" the grandmother asked. With a deep, dark voice, the empress said that the water had torn open her forehead and that the woman must sacrifice her child so that people will never forget that fire comes from the heart of the child.

"Look out the window! There's Moscow!" cried Masha. "Do you see her? That's Moscow, *Moskva!*"

"What have you done?" the grandmother scolded the woman. "Because of you, the whole village is without fire! You must sacrifice your child, otherwise we'll all die of cold!" The mother lamented and wept in despair, but there was nothing she could do.

"Why don't you look out the window? We're finally there!" Masha cried. The train was going slower and slower.

When the child was laid on the hearth, the flames shot up from its heart, and the whole village was lit up so brightly it was as if the Fire Bird had descended to Earth. In the flames the villagers saw the Empress of Fire, who took the child in her arms and vanished with it into the depths of the light.

20

The train arrived in Moscow, and a woman from Intourist walked up to me and said that I had to go home again at once, because my visa was no longer valid. The Frenchman whispered in my ear: "Start shouting that you want to stay here." I screamed so loud that the wall of the station cracked in two. Behind the ruins, I saw a city that looked familiar: it was Tokyo. "Scream louder or you'll never see Moscow!" the Frenchman said, but I couldn't scream any more because my throat was burning and my voice was gone. I saw a pond in the middle of the station and discovered that I was unbearably thirsty. When I drank the water from the pond, my gut began to ache and I immediately lay down on the ground. The water I had drunk grew and grew in my belly and soon it had become a huge sphere of water with the names of thousands of cities written on it. Among them I found her. But already the sphere was beginning to turn and the names all flowed together, becoming completely illegible. I lost her. "Where is she?" I asked, "Where is she?" "But she's right here. Don't you see her?" replied a voice from within my belly. "Come into the water with us!" another voice in my belly cried.

I leapt into the water.

Here stood a high tower, brightly shining with a strange light. Atop this tower sat the Fire Bird, which spat out flaming letters: M, O, S, K, V, A, then these letters were transformed: M became a mother and gave birth to me within my belly. O turned into *omul'* and swam off with S: seahorse. K became a knife and severed my umbilical cord. V had long since become a volcano, at whose peak sat a familiar-looking monster.

But what about A? A became a strange fruit I had never before tasted: an apple. Hadn't my grandmother told me of the serpent's warning never to drink foreign water? But fruit isn't the same as water. Why shouldn't I be allowed to eat foreign fruit? So I bit into the apple and swallowed its juicy flesh. Instantly the mother, the *omul'*, the seahorse, the knife and the volcano with its monster vanished before my eyes. Everything was still and cold. It had never been so cold before in Siberia.

I realized I was standing in the middle of Europe.

III. A GUEST

A GUEST

1

One winter afternoon—I had an ear infection—I walked through an underground passage that led from a subway station to a street with many shops. I had a three o'clock appointment with my ear doctor, whose office was at the end of the street. How late was it? I wondered. Just before the entrance to the passage I'd seen a clock mounted on the side of a kiosk. The clock was missing the numbers three and seven. Beside the clock stood a man who was just taking the missing numbers from his tool kit so as to affix them to the clock's face. The woman inside the kiosk shouted to him how nice it would be to be able to see the correct time again. All at once it seemed strange to me that the numbers were arranged in a circle, since ordinarily numbers are always written from left to right.

As I entered the artificially lit passage, I realized I'd forgotten to check what time it was. It was flea-market day in the passage. The people standing on either side of the aisle inspecting the items offered up for sale looked to me as though they'd come from a dream. Their voices echoed as if from a great distance, and their bodies lacked contours. The night before I had dreamt of a flea, or of a market. When I woke up because of the pain in my ear, I felt as though there was a flea leaping about inside. I remembered a story in which a young woman develops an earache during a coach ride. I can't remember if she was the main character in the story or whether it was only her pain that made me think of her as a heroine. The young woman's mother and lover pour water into the painful ear, shift her head back and forth several times, then pour the water back out. When they do so, a damp flea leaps out of her ear. The woman faints, and her mother screams for help, while her lover seizes the flea—his prey—between his fingertips and pops it into his mouth.

The flea market was like an illustrated encyclopedia. The ground was crowded with small objects made of copper, colored glass, rubber, beech wood, paper, nylon and other materials. On the wall of the passage, which bore several years' worth of posters advertising concerts and demonstrations, a number of jackets and coats were displayed for sale. They had been thoroughly cleaned, some of them even ironed and fitted out with new buttons, but I realized that their previous owners had left behind invisible traces on the clothing. These traces were frightening. It wasn't some contagious illness I was afraid of, but rather the stories of lives unknown to me. A dark gray jacket, for example, which I noticed straight off, reminded me of a neighbor whose life remained a mystery although I'd known him for ten years. He wore a similar jacket, the left pocket of which was pulled slightly out of shape. What did he always carry in it? Every morning he left his apartment, and returned every evening at six o'clock. I knew only the name of the bank he worked for, nothing more. Every so often I noticed, emanating from his apartment, the smell of singed hair.

A hoarse voice addressed me from the left, polite and threatening at once. I shouldn't just look at the jacket, I should try it on. It's true it was a man's jacket, but it would be just right for me. I said nothing and, making no move to touch the jacket, stayed where I was. A short while later a gaunt-looking man with a guitar case appeared. He stopped before the jacket, placed the case on the ground beside him and without the slightest hesitation tried the jacket on. Apparently he was not at all afraid of its former owner. At the time I didn't yet know that even jackets fresh from the factory already have life stories unknown to me and are not like blank paper. The traces are well hidden, but sometimes one can discover them by accident. Once I purchased what appeared in the store to be a perfectly ordinary radio, but at home that night when I turned it on, it emitted a strange noise. The sound resembled the hoarse scream of a male voice. Then there was a brief scratching sound. I inspected the radio with my magnifying glass and discovered in one of the buttons a splinter of fingernail. It was embedded like a fossil in the black plastic. Probably someone working on the assembly line had been attacked by a machine and lost a fingernail, or even a whole finger. The attack was probably classified as an accident. During the quality control check, the finger had been discovered and removed, but no one had noticed the fingernail. I dug it out with my pocketknife and buried it in the garden. Since then, there have been no more inappropriate sounds from my radio.

At a flea market, no one tries to hide the traces hidden in an object. The stuffed animals with their somewhat squashed faces observed me ironically, furiously or disdainfully. Paperback novelettes with faded covers still bore coffee stains and greasy fingerprints from their first readers. The books can never forget their readers, though the readers have no doubt forgotten all about the books' contents. Even more than the traces on these objects, the order in which the items were arranged fascinated me. An iron and a candlestick stood side by side, as though there were some relation between them. I was even able to think how this proximity might be deciphered: the iron produces heat and the candlestick light. Each takes the place of the sun, which from the underground passage is never visible.

The interior of my ear is never illuminated by the sun either. It doesn't want to be illuminated, not even by the ear doctor's artificial light. For eardrums can receive sounds only in the dark. How late was it? Would I still be able to get to the doctor's on time? A pair of ice skates and a clock lay side by side, as though challenging me to guess their relation. I stood before them until I had found a solution: ice skates and clock—both turn in circles. When the skaters twirl on the ice, their skates have to turn with them. When ice skaters twirl, they look like the dolls in music boxes, which you wind like a clock.

At the end of the passage I discovered a book between a black umbrella and a sewing machine with a treadle. I don't know why this book in particular drew my attention. I picked it up, and noticed its slight warmth in the palm of my hand. On the book's cover I saw letters that were written not from left to right, but in a circle. I asked the man who was standing there hawking his wares in what language the book was written, since I don't know of any language whose letters are arranged in a circle. He shrugged his shoulders and said it wasn't a book, it was a mirror. I refused to look at the thing he was calling a mirror.

Maybe it isn't a book, I conceded, but I would still like to know what's going on with this writing.

The man grinned and replied: To our eyes, you look exactly like this writing. That's why I said it was a mirror.

I rubbed my forehead from left to right, as if rewriting my face.

Z

The ear doctor, Dr. Mettinger, had his door half open and was waiting for me in his consulting room. Like all the other doctors who have treated me in this city, he wanted to speak with me alone behind closed doors, as though I had an illness of which no one else should hear. I stopped just before the threshold, unable to take another step, although I was already fairly accustomed to being alone in a room with a strange man, for in this city even the vegetable and fish shops have doors that separate them from the life of the street. I stared at the silver door handle sticking out of the white, smooth door. Surely it will be cold if I touch it, I thought, and then the warmth of my own hand will feel unpleasant. It will be slippery in my moist hand and refuse to let me grip it. The doctor's assistant, observing me from her post at the reception desk, called to me that I was standing in front of the correct room. But I wasn't at all interested in whether it was the right or wrong room.

Come in, Dr. Mettinger said in a peremptory tone. At this, my legs began to march like the legs of a robot. I didn't feel the sort of fear people in this city call claustrophobia. It wasn't the room's enclosedness that troubled me, but rather the strange quiet within it. Unlike the underground passage where I'd seen the flea market, the room had neither sounds nor voices nor superfluous objects, and there was no trace of any of the patients who had been treated here. Since I spent a moment occupied only with gazing around me, Dr. Mettinger withdrew his right hand, which he had been holding out to me.

Have a seat, Ms...

He broke off his sentence and sat down himself at his desk to look for the insurance certificate where he could check my name. As he attempted to pronounce it, I tried to find the best place to put my chair. I didn't want to sit too close to Dr. Mettinger, and pushed the chair a little to the right so I could sit diagonally opposite him. Then I fixed my eyes on his white coat, exactly the way I fix my eyes on a white sheet of paper before I begin to write. I told him I had an earache. As though there were a flea in my ear, I wanted to add, but instead said:

There's a flea living in my ear.

I beg your pardon? Dr. Mettinger asked, looking startled. For a moment, the muscles of his face forgot to hold the individual pieces of flesh together. Dr. Mettinger was not a fat man, but now his flesh appeared superfluous and useless. Why was he startled? Perhaps I had mispronounced the "l" in the word "flea," and Dr. Mettinger had heard an "r." My tongue surreptitiously probed my hard palate to check whether I'd really said an "l." I can distinguish between these two sounds only with my tongue, not with my ears, for my sense of touch is more highly developed with respect to the foreign language than my hearing. My doubt over whether I'd pronounced an "l" vanished again as the doctor asked me where I'd gotten the idea that a flea might be living in my ear. I answered that I knew from a story that such things could happen. He got up abruptly, strode to the window, and shifted a vase of flowers a little to the left so that the sun could shine directly on his desk.

Excuse me, it was a little too dark for me, even though the weather today is splendid, he said in a friendly voice and picked up his big fountain pen. The expression "the weather today is splendid" bothered me for some reason. The fountain pen began writing on a sheet of paper; it was thicker than my thumb and had a middle section that looked like a golden ring.

How long have you had the earache?

I told him I'd woken up in the middle of the night because of a burning sensation in my left ear. On Dr. Mettinger's desk lay three stacks of paper that reflected the sun's glare. The letters vanished in the strong light. While Dr. Mettinger was taking notes, I remembered that the night before I had dreamt of a fire on a sheet of paper. One by one the letters went up in flames, and only the ones containing an enclosed space—like O, P, D, Q and R—remained unharmed. So I hadn't dreamt of the flea or the market after all; I had been mistaken, and only now realized what my dream had really been about.

Dr. Mettinger informed me that he would have to examine my ear. As he spoke, he gazed attentively into my eyes, as if searching for something, though I couldn't imagine what.

Yes, I said uncertainly and turned to the side so he could see my painful ear better.

Uncover the ear, he said in a tone both severe and apprehensive. I pushed back my hair to expose the ear, realizing as I did that my ears were protected by my hair. I hadn't been out with exposed ears at all. How then was it possible for someone to have put something inside my ear that caused me pain? Dr. Mettinger took an instrument that resembled a small telescope or spyglass from a drawer. Then he gazed into my ear with it and held his breath. After a while he began to groan, laid aside his spyglass and said:

You're pregnant.

The doctor's face turned red. I assumed he was furious. A foreigner like me simply showed up at his office, rather than going to a gynecologist, and forced him to make a diagnosis outside his area of expertise. I remembered that this city was full of people who specialized in a particular field and wanted nothing to do with anything else. I couldn't explain to Dr. Mettinger why I'd gone to him and not a gynecologist. Both of us remained silent until I discovered a calendar hanging beside the window. On this calendar, all the days of the year were marked, even this day in December, but there was not a single day on the calendar on which I could have become pregnant. It took me a moment to realize this. The calendar looked strange to me all at once: the dates were arranged in such a way that every month formed a square. Ever since I'd stopped working in an office, I realized, I no longer thought of a month as being square, but rather like a moon, a circular motion which gave my body its orientation. It was no longer important to me whether a day was a Sunday or a Monday.

The numbers on the calendar had to break free of the rows of weekdays, form circles and sketch out moons.

Please look again to be sure if I'm really pregnant; it really isn't possible. Could you have confused a flea with an embryo?

Dr. Mettinger took up his spyglass again and this time poked it deeper into my ear.

What do you see? I asked in a severe tone to overcome my unease.

I see a stage in a theater, he said now in a childish voice.

Try to say more precisely what it is you see. I heard him inhale deeply and then say: I see a building near a harbor, an officer and several women.

The doctor's assistant called to him from outside that he had an important phone call, but he didn't hear her voice.

What do the women standing there look like?

I asked a few more questions, although my curiosity was

abating, for I suspected the doctor of being an inexperienced theater-goer; by the time the women entered, he would see only old, familiar, boring pictures. His voice became somewhat higher as he reported:

The women have on long dresses, silk, what do you call them, oh, that's right, kimonos, and one of them has a knife in her hand. Now she's just plunged it into her belly, a red stain is forming on the white silk, getting bigger and bigger.

I groaned and simply pushed his hand away.

Dr. Mettinger, that is Madame Butterfly, what you describe is not original.

He turned red, and his lips twitched to seize on words which might still be said. But I didn't wait any longer and left his office without saying goodbye.

3

The book I'd bought at the flea market was not a book at all, but rather a box containing four cassette tapes. I ought to have realized this when I saw the circle of letters on the cover. The text turns in a circle, rather than being read from left to right. "A Novel," I read on the title page. Under these words stood the title and the author's name in tiny, indistinct letters.

I inserted the first cassette into my tape recorder and

pressed the button. A female voice began to read from the novel. After a while, I realized I had entered its landscape. Although the plot did not interest me at all, I walked into the novel the way one might mistakenly go into a house that has neither doors nor walls. I hadn't noticed a threshold where I might have paused to consider whether or not I wanted to go in. I began to be afraid of the voice and turned off the tape recorder.

Why couldn't I take pleasure in this voice? After all, I had been looking for a text whose letters would disappear as they were read, like the many novels I read as an adolescent. In those years I went to the neighborhood library almost every day, picked some novel or other and found a seat in a corner of the reading room. My reading was always the same: for the first half hour, I had to struggle against a wall of words. It was strenuous work, but I didn't lose patience, knowing that sooner or later I would gain entrance to the novel. I read and read without knowing why I should be interested in what I was reading and where the novel was taking me. Soon the speed of my reading increased and the letters vanished before my eyes, as during a train ride. When the train accelerates soon after departure, the trees closest to the tracks disappear, and one sees only the distant landscape.

It's been years since I last read a novel in which I could make the letters disappear. This probably has nothing to do with me, but with the city: the only books here are written in a foreign script. As long as I've lived here I've been unable to enter novels. I read and read, but the alphabet never vanishes before my eyes, but rather remains like iron bars or like sand in salad or like the reproduction of my face in the window of a train at night. How often my own reflection in the glass has kept me from enjoying a nocturnal landscape. Even when there was nothing much to see, I would have liked to gaze into the darkness, not at my own mirror image.

Why had it never occurred to me that a tape recording could be the magic means for erasing the letters in a novel? Finally I had succeeded in eliminating the alphabet. I should have been happy.

I turned the tape recorder back on, this time trying to listen to the voice without losing my distance from it. But I couldn't. Either I heard nothing at all, or I was plunged into the novel.

As I turned off the machine, furious, the doorbell rang. It was my new neighbor, who had moved into the building approximately a week ago. I recognized him by the sunglasses that hid his eyes. He asked whether I had a little salt. This was the second time a man had asked me for salt in this city. The first time, a man sitting at the table next to me in a restaurant where only a few tables had salt shakers had asked:

Have you got salt?

He had a cello case and a folding music stand next to him. With his eyes closed, he shook the salt shaker over his salad plate. I thought I could hear the grains of salt falling on the leaves. The man was not afraid to act with his eyes closed. I have often noticed that people carrying musical instruments around with them are not afraid of certain things. I saw on the leaves of his salad white grains of salt which for a moment glittered strangely but soon became transparent.

I filled a teacup with salt for my neighbor and gave it to him. He asked whether I had a visitor. His lips were smooth and slightly moist, though his skin was dry.

No, no one's visiting, I replied, noticing at the same time a voice coming from my kitchen. It was the voice from the tape recorder, which I had already turned off.

I don't have a visitor, but sometimes it happens that there is suddenly a woman here and... I don't mean a woman, but actually just a woman's voice. Because the voice can get in anywhere and . . .

A woman? he asked suspiciously.

No, a voice, not a woman.

He didn't ask any more questions. When I had said goodbye to the neighbor, I returned to the kitchen. The tape recorder was running on its own. I sat down on the chair and pretended the voice wasn't bothering me. I tried to think about the man in sunglasses. "Sunglasses," "professionally," "how old," "thin," "salt," "lips," "tennis shoes" . . . The questions had to be formulated, and they would have to be asked when I saw him again. But I had no idea what I wanted to know about him, what I wanted to think about him, what it was even possible for me to think, for the voice from the tape recorder forced me to return to the novel. The plot was boring, but the voice wouldn't let me go. It determined the temperature of the room in which the novel was set. It determined the smell of the main character's skin. And the figure's gaze was determined by it.

What an incredibly tedious novel, I said aloud, but it didn't help. As if chained down, I sat on the kitchen chair listening to the voice. After the first side of the tape was finished and the tape player turned itself off, the voice went on speaking in my head. I could no longer recognize the words, but the voice itself became clearer and clearer.

That night I made myself a cup of tea and by mistake put salt in it. I had to dump out the tea in the sink. I gazed for a long time into the hole of the drain where the brown spiral of tea was being sucked. I don't know how long I stood there looking at the hole without making a new cup of tea. I was no longer able to measure time, for time passed more quickly when the voice inside me sped up. When it spoke in staccato, time stuttered. Sometimes it stopped, and I took deep breaths so as not to suffocate. At twelve o'clock the voice suddenly vanished. The very same moment, my radio alarm turned on automatically. The news. I ran over and switched the radio off.

4

Once the voice from the tape recorder had taken possession of my life, I became sensitive to every sound from a machine. I noticed, for example, that my typewriter clacked in an irregular rhythm, although the distance between the characters was constant. Only between words did it leave a particularly large space in which a whole character might have fit. But the typewriter fell silent not only between words but at other points as well, and when I listened to the sound while typing I could no longer understand the meaning of the words.

Ty pew r ite r!

The music of this clacking produced a text different

from mine, words incorrectly divided in a stumbling rhythm.

At the time, I regularly wrote short articles that were published as a series in a Japanese women's magazine. When the editor first called me up to ask whether I could write something about holidays in Germany, I immediately said no. I'm not an ethnologist, and have never occupied myself with this sort of topic. The editor said she wasn't looking for scholarly essays but just everyday observations easily understood by her readers. I wound up taking the job for financial reasons. But as soon as I started working on the first article I realized what a difficult task it was. The first topic was birthdays, which are perhaps the most important holidays of all, since even people who try to ignore Christmas like to celebrate their birthdays.

There was a lot for me to write about, since there are many phenomena that interest me, but I was unable to explain any of them. For example, I wrote how a neighbor of mine—although she was already twenty-two years old—was visited on her birthday by her mother, who then hugged and kissed her as though she'd just been born. So the readers of the women's magazine wouldn't get the wrong idea, I added that it was often considered normal here in Germany to kiss one's mother. Even adults are permitted to kiss their mothers, celebrate their own birthdays and receive birthday presents from their mothers. The difference between childhood and adulthood wasn't as clearly demarcated in Europe, I wrote, and then crossed it out. Since I'm not an ethnologist, I wasn't sure I was qualified to make such a statement. If I were an ethnologist, I might have known why birthdays here are so important.

Why do people celebrate birthdays? Because they've lived another year without dying? Here, too, I didn't attempt an explanation, but instead wrote that you weren't allowed to congratulate a person before the actual day of the birthday since this brought bad luck. Then suddenly an explanation for the celebration of birthdays occurred to me. Perhaps people celebrate their birthdays because this is a day when they can distinguish themselves from everyone else. Unlike everyone else, they have a special relationship to this day. People here, I wrote, were in search of ways to distinguish themselves from other people.

Three minutes later I realized many people share the same birthday and crossed out the previous sentence. It also occurred to me that people here like to talk about their zodiac signs. But a sign doesn't belong to a single person; everyone shares his sign with approximately a twelfth of mankind. Thus my supposition that birthdays distinguish people from others couldn't be right. In the end, I wrote: People here like to celebrate their birthdays and talk about signs of the zodiac, especially late at night after a long discussion about politics.

I was dissatisfied with my first article since I hadn't been able to explain any of what I described. The editor, however, said I didn't have to explain anything at all, since there was usually no explanation for superstitions. I promised to write about Christmas the next time, and then about German Unification Day.

Because I didn't have my own typewriter, I often visited Martina, a student who lived across the hall. In a sort of ritual I asked her every time whether by any chance she could work without her typewriter for a few hours. I never saw her writing anything. Nor had she ever mentioned anything about some paper she was working on. Whenever I came to her apartment, she said she wasn't working at the moment because she lacked the necessary calm. Except for a salt shaker on the table, all the objects in her apartment looked as though they'd never been touched. Martina once explained to me that she hardly ever used anything in her apartment since she often slept elsewhere. Nevertheless, I could not understand why her apartment looked like a hotel room that nobody's slept in for months, a hotel room no longer in use because the traces of some unfortunate incident cannot be removed.

Today her alarm clock began to jangle the very moment I was about to pose the usual question. Instead of turning it off, she closed her eyes. I could see her lips moving. It looked as though she were counting numbers soundlessly. After a while she walked over to the alarm clock with deliberate slowness and pressed its button. Finally the clock was silent.

Although I hadn't said a word, she gave me a horrified look, as though I'd reproached her. With both embarrassment and pride she then answered a question I hadn't asked. It was an exercise. She was practicing enduring sounds that seemed to announce catastrophe without being overcome with hysteria or panic.

Once a week Martina went to a therapist. Every sound that leapt into her ears—an alarm clock ringing, the squeal of car brakes, even the voices of strange children on the street—made her think she was no longer able to protect herself from anything.

What do you want to protect yourself against?

Martina did not answer my question. Instead she answered a question I hadn't asked:

No, I don't want to.

I said nothing, and Martina told me that a few days

before she'd been on her way to the subway station and just before she reached the entrance she'd heard a little girl shout: Papa, c'mon!

Martina couldn't see her because the little girl was standing in one of the tunnels at the bottom of the stairs. Martina only heard the voice, and was unable to go down. Then she went home again. She no longer had the strength to visit the girlfriend with whom she'd had a date. The girl's voice had plunged into her ears like an invisible hand grenade and then had exploded silently inside her body. After this incident Martina didn't leave her apartment for three days and didn't talk to anyone.

Carefully I hinted that I, too, had once been possessed by a voice. She had no way of knowing I was describing my current situation. She didn't seem at all interested in the situations of other people. But it wasn't all that bad to be possessed by a voice.

Quite the contrary, I eventually came to take great pleasure in it, I said in an intentionally cheerful tone, which did nothing to change Martina's dour expression. She looked at me, but it was clear she hadn't understood what I'd said. I suggested she always wear her Walkman when she went out so her ears would be protected. She took the Walkman from her desk drawer and tried it to see if it still worked. I asked her whether she'd spoken with our new neighbor yet.

What new neighbor do you mean?

Martina said she hadn't seen any new neighbor.

When I was about to return to my apartment, Martina's boyfriend arrived to pick her up. With his appearance, the oppressiveness in the air vanished. I took a long deep breath. At the same time I missed my tape so badly that I immediately said goodbye to them and went back to my apartment with the typewriter.

I couldn't type a thing that day, nor for many days after, because the voice from the tape recorder became louder and louder, until eventually it drowned out the clacking of the machine. Several times a day I turned off the tape recorder, but it kept turning itself back on.

Don't you want me to write?

For the first time I asked the voice an audible question.

Or do you have something against written characters?

No answer came. I placed my hands on the pause button of the recorder to silence it. Then my radio clock automatically began to speak. I couldn't understand the technical connection between the two machines. News.

I couldn't bear the voice of the clock radio very long, either, though not because I didn't want to hear any other voice but that of the tape player. On the contrary, the radio briefly liberated me from the voice of the novel. From the radio, new voices entered my apartment: the voices of politicians, the voices of dock workers, the voices of men of letters... but I didn't listen for long. I kept returning to the voice of the novel and wasn't sure whether or not I really wanted to escape from it.

5

It was my birthday.

On my desk, ten thin, aching fingers entwined. They had grown out of a tiny hand that, as I realized after a moment, belonged to me. The windows were closed, as is often the case in dreams. But this couldn't have been a dream. Normally in my dreams nothing seems odd to me, nor am I missing anything. Now I was missing all sorts of things. First I poked around a bit with a bent forefinger trying to find my right ear, but I couldn't. Where was my right ear? Had it fallen off the desk?

Where do right ears belong?

In your loins of course, right ears belong in your loins, a voice said to me. I looked for my left ear. It wasn't where it was supposed to be, either. The air was like a mass of kneaded wheat flour. No, it wasn't that the air was heavy, but the voice of a woman had stopped up my ears and kept my eardrums from vibrating.

This voice has plugged up all the holes, I said aloud, for I wasn't sitting alone in the kitchen, I had two companions, Gudrun and her sister. They were busy stirring a bowl of something and didn't hear what I said.

We're almost done, Gudrun said and gave me a worried

glance. Vaguely I remembered having invited ten people to a party. Only I could no longer remember what the occasion was. Gudrun and her sister had arrived an hour early, with no explanation. I was afraid to ask why. Perhaps they already knew I was incapable of receiving guests. Neither of them scolded me when they saw I hadn't yet begun my preparations.

Where's the salt? Gudrun or her sister asked.

I don't have any.

Why don't you have salt?

Gudrun and her sister have almost the same voice so it's impossible for me to tell which one of them is speaking if I don't see their lips. They were talking about how they had too much on their hands these days. One of the two said she couldn't wait for things to calm down around her. That's all she wanted, nothing else interested her any more. Four eyes gazed at me, awaiting my reply. It was as if they wanted to test whether I knew what calm was. And in fact I realized for the first time that, although I knew the meaning of the word "calm," I couldn't really imagine what it might be. I tried to picture a situation in which someone lacked calm. It didn't work. Then I tried to imagine the exact opposite. That didn't work either.

•

If you absolutely have to have salt, I'll go borrow some from my neighbor. That would be OK.

A week ago I had plenty of salt. I gave my neighbor too much salt, that's why I don't have any left.

I heard two women's voices laughing, then I went to my neighbor's apartment and asked whether he could spare some salt. He gazed at me for a moment, and suddenly asked if I'd be interested in working on a project with him. He said he'd give me more details next time. Today he had neither time nor salt for me.

When you yourself were out of salt, I gave you some of mine, I said. To my surprise, my voice came out sounding querulous. A tone I had known only from other women. The neighbor laughed.

Now you sound just like my mother. Don't be like that. Otherwise our project will be a failure.

He laughed again and closed the door.

I had always found it unpleasant to have guests in my apartment. They filled up my rooms with strange sentences I would never have formulated in such a way. Today I found the sound of these sentences particularly unbearable. Sometimes I tried to follow only the sense of the conversation so as not to hear the sounds of the language. But they penetrated my body as though they were inseparable from the sense.

Once, a violent conversation started among a group of people. It was like a wind sock that kept spinning faster and faster. Finally the wind sock swallowed up the people. They were talking about sports, the names of athletes, strikes, matches, points, attacks, kicks. All those present were compelled to speak to defend themselves against the others' words.

At midnight the guests began to dance to disco music. I couldn't hear the music, but saw the wine glasses vibrating. Apparently it was very loud. No one was allowed to miss a beat. The guests weren't dancing at all, they were speaking to one another. When someone stuttered, the others spoke more quickly so the interruption wouldn't be noticed. The rhythm was set by a computerized drum set, just like in disco music. The people breathed, as it were, mechanically, rather than taking irregular breaths whenever they felt like it. My heartbeat and my sighs were ridiculously soft, no match for the powerful speakers. In these black refrigerators, the mass of sounds is frozen. There weren't any speakers in my apartment, and there wasn't any music playing. People were talking. I wanted to transform myself into a stone. Wanted to become a stone like a misplaced comma, to interrupt the clatter of conversation.

Rosa was the only one who paid attention to me. She tried to include me in the conversation as though this were her special task. But I didn't want anyone to talk to me.

Rosa always spoke in an assured tone of voice, a tone

whose existence predated that of Rosa, one which belonged to the city. She had learned it by heart at home or at school, though to this day I am unable to understand how a tone can be learned by heart. Maybe she learned each figure of speech and line of argument in connection with a particular tone. When she spoke in this studied tone, it was rarely possible to object to what she said, for every objection one might make sounded feeble, unnatural, even senseless. I wanted to become a stone and hurl myself against this way of speaking. Then it would either shatter or show a different face.

Does a tone have more than one face? Does a face have more than one tone?

I didn't know anything about Rosa beyond the fact that she had a throat illness which was not apparent when you spoke with her. Her girlfriends had mentioned this throat illness to me several times.

I don't know how this night ended. When I woke up, there was no longer anyone sitting in my apartment. I wasn't even sure whether or not I'd really had guests the night before. Outside a faint dawn bathed the asphalt streets. A few drops of water trickled down the windowpane, as if they wanted to wash away the guests' last fingerprints.

When I went to the bakery to buy breakfast rolls, I saw Rosa. I called her name, although I didn't have anything in particular to say to her. She groaned before I could utter another word and gave a nervous smile. She pressed her paper bag of rolls against her chest and turned her back on me. As she left the bakery she said to me—though I hadn't asked—that she had no time today.

I'm under time pressure. I'm not going to have a minute of calm all week, since I have so much on my hands. But next week I'll give you a call, she shouted from the street into the bakery where I was still standing. Why did she want to call? Besides, it wasn't possible to call me. She was gone before I could tell her I didn't have a telephone.

6

I undressed, lay down and closed my eyes.

Whenever I felt ill, I would simply lie like this for several days, rather than going to a doctor or buying medicine. I was afraid of taking medicine, even home remedies like hot currant juice with honey to ward off colds. Fighting an illness seemed to me to show a lack of respect. Once it arrived, there was nothing to do but cooperate and accept it.

Sometimes I tried to see the voice, too, as an illness and behave accordingly. But—unlike with other illnesses—I didn't want it to leave me for good one day.

When night fell, I tried to locate parts of my body with

which I could perceive the voice. I didn't think I was feeling it on my eardrum like an ordinary voice. Especially when I was lying down it came to me in a surprising way. First it stroked my neck cautiously. This tended to go on too long for my taste, and I was also afraid it might elegantly strangle me. I never understood what it wanted from me, if it wanted anything at all. Nor could I ask it any questions, since it couldn't hear. It was a voice without ears.

Sometimes I allowed it to caress me for hours, my belly, the soles of my feet, my nose, breasts, fingertips, thighs. Fortunately I was not obliged to show any reaction, the voice did not expect this of me. I didn't have to formulate a single sentence, and was able to transform myself into pure tactile sensation, a sense of touch without language. Not only spoken language, but body language as well had become superfluous. I felt liberated from the gaze of others as well, for it was a voice without eyes.

To my surprise, however, when I went outside I realized I was not liberated from every gaze. This time I met Rosa in front of the post office. She asked if I wanted to come over for a cup of tea because she wanted to show me her new apartment which she'd only just moved into. I had never found the furnishings of apartments particularly interesting, though it occurred to me that I could write an article for the magazine about this since the furnishings of an apartment not only pose financial and practical problems, but also have a religious aspect.

That would be very nice, I said. Though at once I felt guilty. There was something inhuman about being interested only in things I could observe like an ethnologist.

The moment I entered the apartment, Rosa peered deep into my eyes, as though she wanted to see exactly what sort of reflection her apartment made in them. Right away I was required to decide whether or not I found her apartment attractive, which was impossible for me to do since I can't form an opinion of an apartment I don't live in. All the same, Rosa seemed to want to read some judgment in my eyes. Perhaps it was an exercise for her: seeing her own apartment with a stranger's eyes and assigning it grades that would later help her improve it. Perhaps for her this apartment was something like a self-portrait: the furniture, posters, rug, writing implements, stereo joined together to illustrate her personality. But why did she want me to see it?

I kept running into a wall of questions as to the point of it all. For me, my apartment had the function of a skin. No one could observe it from the inside. I always found it unpleasant to see people in my apartment, and even more unpleasant when they observed it with curiosity. My apartment doesn't want to be given a grade, otherwise it cramps up. I want it to be all but invisible. It isn't there to be shown off, nor to represent any sort of accomplishment. It cannot be either attractive or ugly, since it isn't there to be looked at in the first place. Rosa asked me hesitantly what I was up to these days. She couldn't imagine me having a professional career or a relationship that took up a great deal of time.

I've been listening to a voice that does not resonate in any body, I replied.

Rosa came closer.

What sort of voice?

The voice of a woman.

Rosa was immediately disappointed with my answer. Not wanting to be impolite, though, she made a joke instead of showing her disappointment directly.

I keep hearing a woman's voice, too, one that tells me all the times I keep doing something wrong. But I know perfectly well whose voice it is.

7

I placed a classified ad in a newspaper. Anyone who read the ad was supposed to get the impression that for sentimental reasons an old woman was looking for an old novel she had enjoyed reading sixty years before. That this old woman was willing to pay one hundred marks for a book that had value neither for a passionate lover of literature nor a book collector might have seemed somewhat unusual. So at first I was afraid my request would be an odd bird fluttering garishly away between the neat columns of classifieds, and that a few readers would call me up just out of curiosity. But when I read other advertisements on the same page, I realized how inconspicuous mine was. For example, one woman wrote that she was prepared to pay two hundred and fifty for a goldfish that resembled her dead son. And a wealthy man was looking for a woman with only one ear, for purposes of marriage. In comparison, my desire to purchase an old novel for one hundred marks was relatively modest. More precisely, I wanted not the novel but the book. The novel didn't interest me. I wanted to own the book in order to lock the voice from the tape behind the bars of the printed letters.

A few days later a student called me and said he had the book I was looking for but unfortunately couldn't sell it to me because it was connected with certain personal memories that were very important to him. If I really wanted to see the book, though, he would visit me and bring it with him.

Three days later he appeared. The book's title page had a dark red color that struck me as familiar. Hadn't I once known someone who wore a shirt with a similar color? The title page bore no heading. The book's owner explained that the title had no doubt stood on a separate leaf which had probably become detached from the book and eventually gotten lost. In the middle of the page stood a drawing of a clock. It was missing not only its hands, but also two numbers: three and seven. The book was much thinner than I had imagined it. How could a novel that refused to come to an end live in this little book? I told my visitor I'd been looking for this book for a long time, and until now I'd known only its title, author's name and contents. I didn't mention the tapes. It would have been difficult to explain why I was so eager to own the novel as a book when I already had the tapes in my possession.

So what is it you do in this city? the owner of the book asked me. I looked at him for the first time. His lips kept moving after he'd finished his sentence.

Usually I sit at the window and listen to the voice of a woman.

As soon as I said the word "voice," I immediately remembered that I hadn't wanted to mention the tapes. But the man didn't ask any more questions. Instead he looked at my fingers, which were trembling. I placed the coffee cup, which I'd been trying to lift, back on the table.

See this?

He turned the book over and drew my attention to the greasy fingerprints on its back cover.

That doesn't bother me, I replied, without quite knowing why he was showing me the marks. I opened the book.

When I stared at the two open pages, my eyes were incapable of reading even a single sentence. He asked again:

Did you see the fingerprints?

I closed the book, inspected the marks on its back cover and tried to discover what was special about them. The man's name was Simon. Although I hadn't asked him, he told me his name.

Go on reading. After all, you wanted to read the book. I can stay here until you're finished. But, as I said, I can't sell you the book, because of the fingerprints.

Once more I studied the form of the five fingertips visible on the red paper. Simon laughed and showed me his right hand. His middle finger was missing.

I read the novel before I lost my middle finger working in a factory, and this is the only image my finger left behind. I don't even have a photograph of it. That's why I don't want to sell you the book.

I opened the book again. It seemed to me as if the voice became quieter when the book was open. I didn't have the courage to ask Simon whether he, too, could hear this. I couldn't even ask whether he heard the voice at all. He sat there calmly and went on saying:

Take your time and read the book, all of it. I'll stay here until you're finished.

•

An hour passed without my having read anything. I recognized individual letters, but couldn't make words out of them, as if the book were written in a language I didn't know. It got dark. I couldn't bring myself to part from the book; every time I opened it, the voice lost its strength. I wondered if I should ask Simon to visit me every day with the book. But sooner or later he'd have to go home.

Although I couldn't read the book, I kept flipping through it. I had to be careful not to flip too quickly or too slowly. Otherwise, Simon might have noticed I wasn't reading at all. Simon sat on a kitchen chair. From time to time he lit a cigarette and smoked with eyes half closed. He held the cigarette between his thumb and ring finger. He held his index finger in the air, pointing meaninglessly in some direction. At some point Simon silently walked over to the sofa, lay down and fell asleep. I closed the curtains and covered his body with a woolen blanket. There were no more street sounds any longer. It was a night with a greenish full moon.

I stood for a while on the balcony looking at the moon. The shadows on its surface could be read neither like numbers nor letters. They resembled no signs known to me. Once I had thought the cycles of the moon determined my sense of life, but now it was a flat shape. Through the window I could already see the first light of dawn. I kept turning pages in the book, playing the role of a passionate reader, although Simon had long since fallen asleep. He wouldn't have checked to see if I was still reading in any case. He just wanted to give me a chance to see the novel with my own eyes.

When Simon woke up, I had to tell him I hadn't made any progress reading the book because my eyes couldn't make words out of the letters. I didn't know if Simon understood me or not. He only repeated that he would stay until I finished reading the book. He stayed all day. Once he left the house without saying anything, and I thought he wasn't coming back. But half an hour later he returned with a large plastic bag from which he produced vegetables, bread, cheese, wine and cigarettes. He stayed the next day, too, and the days thereafter.

I had laid the book open on the table in front of me.

The voice from the tape player became weaker every day, but I still couldn't make any progress reading. My abdomen began to ache. I didn't know whether or not the pain had anything to do with the disappearance of the voice. At times I hoped Simon would leave the apartment with the book so the voice would return. But just as often I hoped Simon would never leave, so that the book, too, would remain. But then the pain in my abdomen would remain as well, and I might have to go to the doctor. I imagined an ear doctor or gynecologist might be able to invent some reason for my pain.

8

Where are you going? my neighbor asked, not even bothering to say hello first, when I ran into him on the stairs.

I wanted to run down to the pharmacy for some painkillers. For several days now—I wasn't sure how long—I hadn't left the apartment, since Simon brought me everything I needed. But the painkillers I wanted to get myself, without his knowing; I had never before taken pills of any sort, and it seemed to me almost like a crime.

The neighbor's question had a threatening ring to it. I couldn't answer. For a moment the two of us stood there silently on the stairs. His eyes were hidden behind his sunglasses. His dark red shirt looked familiar to me. After a while he extracted a small metal object from his trouser pocket and held it up before my eyes. It was a key. When I tried to seize it, he quickly returned it to his pocket. I started down the stairs and heard him say behind me in a commanding tone: Come see me tonight. I have to talk to you. Seven o'clock.

It had been a long time since I'd spoken with anyone except

Simon. I no longer felt the need to visit acquaintances to confirm my acquaintance with them, nor to make the acquaintance of people I didn't yet know. Whether or not I knew someone no longer had any importance. The author of the novel was the only person whose acquaintance I'd have liked to make. I looked in the phone book and discovered thirteen women with her name. I could have called up all thirteen and asked each of them whether she'd written the novel. This would have been worth the effort if I'd known for certain that one of the thirteen was the author, but it was unlikely that the author and I lived in the same city. Actually I didn't really want to meet her. I wasn't interested in the person who had written this boring novel. What aroused my interest was my suspicion that the speaker on the tape was in fact the author. The only series of books-on-tape I knew was called "The Authors Read," and the reader on the tape seemed too unprofessional to be a trained actress. But I kept thinking about the voice's owner. I wanted to find her, to hear what the voice sounded like when it came from a body, not an electrical apparatus.

I told Simon about neither my tapes nor my neighbor. Simon probably took me for a lonely woman with no friends in this city who occupied herself only with reading and writing. In reality, I was able neither to read nor write. I sat at my desk, upon which lay a book and a stack of manuscript pages, and did nothing. Since Simon had moved in, I hadn't been able to write anything at all. It was strange for me to have gone so long without writing. From time to time I distinctly felt the urge simply to set down letters on a sheet of paper, but this urge vanished as soon as I glanced at the open book. I lost my way among its letters as if in a forest. Perhaps I needed the voice from the tape recorder to be able to write again.

When I wasn't at my desk, I sat with Simon at the window, watching the people who passed by the building. Most of their faces were uninteresting, but a few of them I observed attentively because they could be connected with a particular number. For example, I said to Simon, a boy walking past looked like three, not because he walked stooped over so that his spine formed the shape of this number; nor because he might have answered three out of five questions on his last quiz in school. The mouth of the boy was shaped in such a way as if he were about to pronounce the word "three," but this wasn't the reason either. I didn't tell Simon what the reason was. Simon said I saw the city as a clock, perhaps because I had lost all sense of time.

But I was still able to tell time, otherwise I wouldn't have been able to appear at my neighbor's door at exactly seven o'clock.

You're punctual. That's a good sign, he said, and grinned.

He was wearing the dark red shirt. Soon the color of the wool shirt assumed a certain autonomy and began to float back and forth in my field of vision. I could see nothing else but this color, and suddenly it occurred to me why it looked so familiar. It was the color of the book Simon had brought me, the color of the novel.

The neighbor offered me a cup of tea. His voice now was soft and indistinct. The threatening tone in which he'd spoken a few hours before was gone. Since I didn't know what to say, I asked him what profession he was in. He blinked. This time he wasn't wearing his sunglasses. His eyes had no shape, they consisted of a continual opening and closing.

He replied that he was currently unemployed. The business he'd founded together with his girlfriend had gone bankrupt, though he now had a plan that might well be successful. He'd had his telephone cut off so his girlfriend couldn't call him any more, for there was nothing he found more unbearable than her voice. After he had thoroughly and maliciously described his girlfriend, he suddenly asked if I meditated often. Caught off guard, I replied:

Yes, no, I mean, if I say yes it already means no.

I never spoke the word "meditation" aloud, since meditation described, comprehended and presented as such wasn't meditation at all. I meditated only in an overcrowded subway, or in a department store in front of a display table heaped with sale items. I meditated standing up and with open eyes. I meditated often. The idea of achieving a state of calm or even discovering one's true nature through meditation was utterly foreign to me. Rather, I would lapse into meditation when I was fascinated by large crowds of people or mountains of industrial products. They fascinated me because when I looked at them I felt certain I could just as easily do without them.

I told the neighbor everything I could think of on the subject of meditation. He put on his sunglasses and listened. I didn't have the impression he understood what I was saying. He didn't ask any questions, either. Perhaps my words lacked all importance to him. After a while he asked whether I talked in my sleep.

How should I know? In any case, I've never been woken up by my own voice, only by that of another woman.

Ask Simon whether you've talked in your sleep. Don't forget to ask him soon, because he can't stay with you much longer. Perhaps it's already too late. He may already have left. The neighbor's fingers were bony and conspicuously long. I noticed this when—after finishing his tea—he placed his hands on the table.

How did you know he's been staying with me and that

his name is Simon? I asked, trying not to move any part of my body.

The clock showed exactly ten o'clock. Cautiously I asked the neighbor what his name was, for he didn't have a name plate on his door. It had only just occurred to me that I didn't know his name. He said, grinning, that his name was Z.

That can't be your name. You can't expect me to believe your name is an abbreviation of zero just because it's zero minutes after ten.

Then I have a different name, he said, sounding exhausted, but didn't say what it was.

The next morning Z was still there. His face was now completely different. The shape of his eyes was distinct, and he didn't blink as often. The flesh of his stomach had grown overnight. I realized I was afraid of him. When I asked him whether he would prefer to drink coffee or tea, he replied:

I never drink tea.

But I clearly remembered him drinking tea once because he had put salt in his tea by mistake. I just couldn't make up my mind when this had occurred.

•

I went into the kitchen to make coffee. I tried to avoid putting an unpleasant suspicion into words. But I couldn't get past the ridiculous question of whether this was the same man I had visited the day before. Hadn't we both been in his apartment yesterday? Why had we woken up in mine? Where was Simon? Perhaps it wasn't important whether he was the same man as the one from yesterday or not. In any case, I hardly knew him. I knew only that he was my neighbor and that he wanted me to call him Z. No one can really have the name Z, but anyone can ask people to call him anything. So the name Z was not a way to recognize him.

But where was Simon? And where was his book? It no longer lay on my table. The water was boiling in the kettle I'd purchased at a department store. A thermos bottle, two pots and three soup ladles lying near the kettle presented themselves to me. I tried to put these objects together in my head to paint the picture of a kitchen that held a comfortable place for me. But it didn't work. Individual objects kept hovering out of context before my eyes. What was the point of this kettle, these bowls and these forks? What was that round metal shape, this wooden rectangle? Why had I assembled them in this room? I sat down on the kitchen chair where Simon had often sat. For the first time I noticed the flower-patterned wall, an unpleasant sight. How long had I had this wallpaper? Why had I never tried to take it down? To my surprise, the kettle had the same pattern as the wallpaper. I drew the conclusion that both were manufactured by the same company. If I had seen the kettle at the flea market beside a fountain pen, I might have seen a different relationship between the objects. A kettle and a fountain pen each have an entrance through which something can go in and—unlike the human ear—an exit through which it can come out again. There was still an early-morning light outside. In the glow of the kitchen lamp, white coffee cups gleamed dimly. I remembered that in the novel a scene like this one had been described to express a certain emotion on the part of a character. I hated that part of the text. Fortunately, I could no longer remember the emotion that was being described.

Both the voice of the novel and the book were gone. They had both lost all importance for my life, but all the same I had the unfamiliar feeling that I could no longer feel at ease without them.

At breakfast, Z said to me that he wanted to go on observing Martina. I was surprised he knew her. He also knew I was using her typewriter.

She doesn't interest me, I said.

That doesn't make her uninteresting, he replied calmly.

What's so special about her?

My voice was loud. He grinned out of one side of his mouth.

Nothing at all. She has a problem that probably affects millions of women. We have to take an interest in such problems if we wish to be successful.

9

At three in the afternoon, Z left my apartment. I stood empty-handed at the window and realized my hands needed something to hold on to. For example, the keys of the typewriter, a book or the hands of another person. Since the day Simon first came to visit me, I hadn't written a single word, not even a letter. I wanted to write again, but didn't know what. My fingers kept searching for the keys.

I went to Martina's apartment to ask whether she could lend me her typewriter for a little while.

She opened the door red-eyed and told me that a bus driver had shouted at her the day before. Until then she'd been doing quite well. She'd been walking around with her Walkman as usual and when she got on the bus she noticed that the bus driver was opening and closing his mouth like a goldfish, turning redder and redder. Surprised, she took off her headphones. As soon as she did so, a sharp voice pierced her ears.

Can't you read? Are you illiterate?

Martina still didn't understand what he was talking about. If he'd asked if she couldn't hear, she'd have understood, but not if she couldn't read. Then an older woman standing behind her took Martina by the back of her jacket and pulled her out of the bus. She pointed her index finger at a sign affixed to the bus.

After 7:00 p.m. show all passes when entering bus, the woman read to her in a loud, clear voice like an elementary school teacher. Martina said quietly: I know how to read.

This made the bus driver even angrier:

Everyone who breaks laws is illiterate. I don't mean that all illiterates are law-breakers, but every law is written down somewhere, that's for sure, and...

After this incident Martina spent three days in bed without eating.

You ought to shield your eyes as well, then nothing can happen to you. For instance, you could always hold a book in front of your face, I said to comfort her.

Martina didn't say anything. After a while she went into the kitchen, placed her hands on the handle of the kettle and began to cry. When the palms of a person's hands touch something warm, it sometimes happens that the person's feelings melt and spill out of her mouth. I knew there was a similar scene in the missing novel. The scene involved a woman who cried several times during the novel. I was glad I couldn't remember her life story any more.

I visited our new neighbor the day before yesterday, Martina said all at once. He said he used to study psychology. Maybe he can help me.

Martina blew her nose, which made her appear to be smiling. I stood up because I didn't want to hear anything more about the neighbor. It wasn't clear to me why he had told Martina about his studies.

The typewriter's over there. You can go on writing your novel, Martina said in a disinterested voice, gesturing with her chin in the direction I was already looking. Immediately, I was filled with hatred for the word "novel."

I'm not writing a novel, I said, horrified, and Martina looked at me in surprise.

That evening it began to rain. I sat at the typewriter, hitting the Z key over and over. I found the shape of this letter unappealing, but my fingers insisted on typing, and since I couldn't think of a single sentence, I had no choice but to keep typing the same letter again and again.

Why haven't you come? I told you to come, I said aloud. Suddenly it occurred to me whom I was talking to. Simon was gone, and Z wasn't in the apartment either. There was nothing to stop the voice from returning. Without it, I thought, I would never be able to formulate a sentence again.

Z one

Z ither

Z ero

I typed the letter Z separately from the rest of the word.

Gradually the keys of the typewriter began to feel lighter. I left the Z out:

one
ither
ero
I couldn't stop typing:
inc
enith
ygote
ephyr
ealot
ombie
ed

I typed and typed, not noticing that the door had opened. Z stood there, coughing. When he took my hands, they lost all desire to type.

For some reason I can't seem to write anything at all today, I said before he had time to ask.

10

The next day the voice of the novel returned to me.

As if in a trance, I typed an endless chain of Z-less words. Then I took a new sheet of paper and typed a row of Zs.

When I tore up the page and threw it into the wastepaper basket, I heard a woman's voice behind me. At first I thought someone was talking on the street. Then I realized it was the voice of the novel, for I heard it not with my eardrums but with some other part of my body I was unable to localize. When I closed the lid of the typewriter, the voice became more distinct. I slipped into bed and turned out the light. I remained lying there—I don't know how long—and didn't notice when the door opened and Z appeared beside my bed.

Are you sleeping?

The voice disappeared when Z spoke, and my sense of hearing was immediately restricted to my eardrums.

No, I'm not asleep.

What are you doing if you aren't sleeping?

I went on lying there like a stone and gave no answer. I was afraid that Z, too, had heard the woman's voice and would call me a traitor. But why? Why shouldn't I listen to the voice? Z scrutinized my face like a doctor looking for a mark on my skin. I myself could not feel my own body, though gradually I was able to perceive the voice again. It was as if the room contracted when it spoke more quickly. When the voice grew louder, the room expanded and then existed only as the voice. In this room created by the voice, I could not find my own body. The room was empty and had neither walls nor furniture. It consisted only of a voice. Didn't it resemble the apartment I'd wished for?

•

Time passed. I awoke from the sleep that was not sleep and saw that an alarm clock and Z were lying beside me. I had never before seen anything in such extreme proximity. Z, who woke up shortly afterward, picked up the clock and shook it like a salt shaker. Then he asked me once more if I was asleep. When I said no, he asked why I was lying there like a stone. I sat up and found my arms and head much heavier than before. I could hear the voice only in my head. On the small table next to the bed lay a stone. I picked it up and shook it several times, the way you shake a salt shaker. The stone made a strange sound. Was it hollow on the inside? Z stood up and started walking back and forth in the room. I said to him:

I've always wanted to become a stone. Besides, I'm still sick.

Z smiled as if in relief. Most likely he'd thought I was bored with him. I wasn't really sick, but since otherwise it wouldn't have been acceptable for me to imitate a stone, I decided to be sick. It occurred to me that I might really be sick.

I have an ear infection. I keep hearing a woman's voice. It's because of the infection, you see.

Z grinned, took my hand and said:

I know. I know everything. But we'll have to be thrifty

with our speech and use our heads. Don't tell anyone you're sick. Don't call your illness "ear infection." "Ear infection" sounds ridiculous. You mustn't ever say anything ridiculous about yourself. Don't talk with other women about the voice. I'll tell you next week where our work goes from here. I have to go away for a week to collect the materials for the project. In the meantime, don't speak to anyone. Stay here alone until I come back. I told you right from the start that I'm planning a project. And this project can be completed only with your help.

The next day I went downtown to buy a typewriter. Since I couldn't visit Martina any longer, I needed one of my own. I would have to turn in another article for my series in the Japanese magazine soon. The deadline was approaching, and I felt as if I would be able to write again. Moreover, now that Z was gone, the voice had returned as well.

I went to a big department store downtown. While I was comparing various typewriters and studying the brochures, I remembered what Martina had said to me. She thought I was writing a novel. My hatred for the word "novel" flared up again. Of course "novel" is only a sort of product label, like "typewriter," and a book has to be called "novel" or "stories" or "poems," since if you can't categorize it in some way it's impossible to decide on the size of the print run, the target audience, marketing strategies and price. Therefore the word was very important. I hated it all the same.

How nice it would have been if the voice hadn't belonged to a novel. I couldn't understand why it had picked something so boring to attach itself to. Perhaps the voice found it satisfying not to have to live in a short text. Most readers don't like to read short texts because they have so little time. They would rather go for a walk in a long novel and not have to change. The short texts would go for a walk inside their bodies, which they would find exhausting.

When I came home with the new typewriter and began to type, I suddenly felt quite attracted to the word "ethnology." It no longer surprised me that I couldn't manage to take an interest in romances or adventure novels. I would much rather write short reports on the inhabitants of this city. And if I didn't succeed, I would write nothing but single letters of the alphabet.

I wrote the letter Z ten times on a sheet of paper and then destroyed it. When I stared at the second white sheet, I suddenly felt as if I would now be able to write something I had never before written.

11

Martina sat, eyes closed, on the floor of her apartment.

Inhale deeply three times, Z's voice said. Although Martina's eyes were closed, you could tell by her expression that she was trying to meet his eyes. Whenever he looked at her, she smiled. I had never seen her face so radiant.

And exhale slowly seven times.

Z's powerful voice pierced my ears as well. Martina inhaled and exhaled according to his instructions. Z took her arms and moved them slowly, first to the left, then to the right, and finally above her head. Rigid and yielding at the same time, like a doll, she assumed various positions. She seemed to be convinced of some idea I knew nothing about. After a while the room grew dark. Martina's bare arms and chest gave off a faint glow. In the background one could see the shadow of the curtain.

I feel better, she said. I lay like a trough beside Z. Although he'd forbidden me to do so, I had opened my eyes just a crack and was watching Martina. Z explained something to her in a gentle voice. Martina began to move as though she were quickly taking off a shirt that was much too tight and clung to her skin. She threw the piece of clothing she'd removed in my direction. In reality she wasn't wearing anything at all. My supine body received the invisible clothing. It didn't hurt, it didn't make me happy. I went on lying there as Z had instructed me and tried to breathe as little as possible. It wasn't difficult to do, as I felt like a stone.

That wasn't bad, Z said to me in a business-like tone after the first of his consultations. I hadn't understood what I was doing with Martina, and couldn't ask. Perhaps I didn't want to know.

The next day a woman I had never seen before came for a consultation with Z. Although I couldn't see the woman's face because of the way my body was positioned, I realized at once that she felt Z's gaze all over her body and was enjoying it like a sort of shower. Soon she, too, began to move in the same way I'd already observed with Martina, as if she were pulling off a piece of clothing and tossing it in my direction. It didn't hurt, just felt strange, as if I'd been sent to some other place, even though I was still in the room with the woman and Z. In this other place, I wasn't lonely, just alone. There were a number of voices there. Not only the voice of the novel, but many other voices as well surrounded my body. After the woman left the room, Z placed one hundred marks on my desk and without a word left the apartment.

The next day a third woman arrived. She had a hoarse voice that was not hers but belonged to a different, older woman. She was possessed by this stranger's voice and suffered from it as if from an illness. It was as if she was unable to assemble the words she wished to speak, and therefore spoke quite poorly. No wonder: when there's always another voice interrupting, you immediately forget how you wanted to end your sentence. When the woman sat down in front of Z and closed her eyes, Z looked at her until her expression melted. Everything was strangely still. Then she took off an invisible garment and threw it on my body. An hour later the woman had a high, clear voice that instantly aroused my pity.

What a lovely stone, she said to Z as she was leaving, meaning me. For years I had dreamt of becoming a stone.

One day Rosa came for a consultation. I didn't know how Z advertised his services. Sometimes women I knew came, sometimes women I didn't know. But no one recognized me because I had plastered my face with light-gray, concrete-like paint. My nose and mouth looked like two hillocks, and my eyes were holes. On my cheeks, Z wrote the numbers three and seven. When the women arrived, they generally gave my face a brief glance and acted as if they hadn't seen anything.

That looks like a clock made of stone, Rosa said when she saw me.

When she met me at the bakery the next morning, she said hello in a friendly voice and told me that her sore throat had disappeared when she started going to meditation. I was so surprised to hear the word "meditation" that I was unable to answer.

I can also sleep well now that I'm in meditation. I used to hear a piercing voice in my dreams all night long. Now it's gone, and I've found my way back to my true self.

The next day I brought this up with Z and asked him not to use these expressions.

Why do you use words like that?

What words do you mean?

"Meditation," for example.

What's wrong with it?

Don't you get goose bumps on your lips when you say it? I don't mean there's anything wrong with meditation, but the word . . .

Z didn't listen. He was convinced he could liberate these women from their sleepless nights and illnesses. He thought he knew what methods and words could best help him reach his goal.

12

More and more women came for consultations. Almost every day I had to lie down next to Z and remain motionless for two or three hours. I tried not to listen to Z's voice.

Nevertheless, individual sentences or groups of sentences sometimes sprang into my ears. Then it was impossible to keep my body still. My fingers tapped lightly on the floor, or my belly quivered. Z didn't seem to notice his sentences displeased me. He gained immediate control over each of the women, who were overcome with a mixture of fear and respect whenever Z spoke or stared at them in silence. At first the women hid the fact that they were strangely shaken. They sat there with disapproving expressions on their faces until their fear took over. Once they told him something, trembling and sometimes even weeping, they calmed down. But the flesh of their faces remained stiff. I never heard anyone laugh in Z's presence.

Once it became too much for me. I began to laugh, quietly but perceptibly, when I heard Z tell a woman he could liberate her by killing the voice of her mother. This voice, he said, lived in the woman's body and was consuming all her strength. When the woman nodded obediently, I couldn't help laughing. Fury and pleasure released my petrified stomach muscles. Then I had to speak to fight back the fear that suddenly filled me.

I wouldn't kill the voice of the mother. I would sleep with it. That would be incest in its most beautiful form.

The woman looked at me, horrified, as though she'd seen a stone that could speak. Z immediately turned on the tape recorder. Meditative music erased the disharmony I had created in the atmosphere of the room.

After the woman had left, Z offered to start paying me two hundred marks per day instead of one. Apparently he saw my laughter as a kind of blackmail.

But what do you need me for? You can go on playing your game without me. I quit, I said, without even stopping to think about the money.

No, I can't do it alone. I need a body to receive the left-over voices, otherwise the therapy won't work, he replied.

I'm not a garbage can.

But for you, if I understand correctly, these voices are not garbage.

I said nothing.

You can earn money and help these women at the same time. That's not such a bad thing, is it? he said gently, placing his hand on mine.

I had never before thought about wanting to help women. I couldn't explain why the whole idea seemed so absurd to me. And I wasn't convinced the women felt better after their consultations. It's true most of them said they felt much better after the treatment, but to me they looked as if Z had broken one of their bones.

This bone might be a tiny, insignificant one, perhaps so tiny no one even knows it exists. Its location and function are possibly unknown, and no one has tried to find it. Nevertheless, one can clearly see when this bone has been broken.

Sometimes I even see a woman walking down the street in broad daylight with a broken bone. She can be well-dressed or wearing heavy makeup, she can be in good spirits or seated in the protective armor of an automobile, but still I can see she's had this particular bone broken. Which doesn't necessarily mean she's been treated by Z. I see too many women with broken bones for this to be possible. There must be many many people performing the same service, though to this day I don't know exactly what it is Z does. He speaks with women, or stares at them in silence. That's all I can make out.

When I wake up in the middle of the night, I often feel the need to write something down. I sit at my desk and hold my fingers above the typewriter until I can remember the clattering sound I once knew. It's no longer possible for me to write something about a particular subject. Often I even have difficulty putting together coherent sentences.

When I am incapable of writing even a sentence, I simply type the words that occur to me of their own accord. I divide them up incorrectly:

Maga z ine

Fro z en

Reali z ation

When I look at the page the next day, I find only a series

of meaningless words and no longer know what it was I wanted to notate. Writing these broken words is the only activity that calms me. Then I pick up the full page and hold it in my hand, satisfied, as if I've notated something important.

Un z ip
Pri z e
Hori z on
Sei z e
Ha z y
Mesmeri z e
Recogni z e
Ga z e
Da z z led
Z ig z ag